THE WHITE STAG ADVENTURE

The White Stag Adventure

RENNIE McOWAN

RICHARD DREW PUBLISHING

GLASGOW

First published 1986 by
Richard Drew Publishing Ltd.,
6 Clairmont Gardens, Glasgow G3 7LW
Scotland

British Library Cataloguing in Publication Data

McOwan, Rennie
  The white stag adventure.
  I. Title
  823'.914[J]   PZ7

ISBN 0-86267-166-3

Set in Italian Old Style by John Swain Ltd., Glasgow
Printed and bound in Great Britain
by Cox & Wyman, Reading

For Lesley, Michael, Tom and Niall,
now grown up

Contents

Author's Note

The children in this book, Gavin and his friends Clare, Michael and Mot, first appeared in *Light on Dumyat*, published by the Saint Andrew Press in 1982. Mot is actually Tom, but as a very young boy he wrote his name backwards and it stuck as a nickname.

CHAPTER 1

The Castle in the Lochan

The deer were uneasy, standing with heads high, tension-filled, in the dark of the Highland night. The men were also uneasy as they picked up their rifles and pulled Balaclava helmets over their faces, leaving only their eyes and mouths free.

For a quivering second each side sensed the presence of the other. Then, suddenly, car headlights blazed on and dazzling beams of light shot across the moor, outlining the deer against the black night as if in some etched drawing, their eyes glittering and shining.

They did not move because the thunderclap of the blaze of light rocked their senses and by the time they had recovered it was too late.

Rifles spat fire from the car, the noise of the shots reverberated into the darkness, striking the rocks on the hillsides in Glen Dochart and echoing in the corries where fox and eagle shrank closer into den and nest as they heard the sounds of death.

The clean scents of moorland after rain were clouded with the smell of explosive bullets. Four deer fell dead, one in a wounded, kicking heap. One, mortally struck, sped off into the night and, in pain, limped its way over the hills by the old pass near Creaig nan Eirannach, the Rock of the Irishman, to the long glen of Balquhidder and then by Glen Buckie and onwards yet until it lay down finally on the lower slopes of Ben Ledi, never to rise again.

Suddenly, shouts of alarm rang out as the men got out of the car to pick up the corpses.

Out of the darkness came a large stag, with sweeping antlers, looking in the headlights like some gigantic beast from mythology, white and ghost-like. It bore down on them, angry and menacing.

'Look out!' yelled one man, frantically trying to level his rifle. Others swore and one got off a wild shot. The stag leapt the bonnet of the car and bounded off into the darkness, its white, disappearing shape followed by a fusillade of shots.

'Did you see that?' said one angrily. 'What a size of a beast! And it was white! It came right at us! I've never seen that before.'

Another chuckled grimly. 'I thought it was a ghost! It's got a charmed life anyway. Fear makes them rush in panic!

'But we'll keep an eye out for it next time. It's the only white stag I've heard of. It would be worth a lot stuffed or caught alive.'

They began to load the corpses, still muttering about the white stag. 'Get a move on,' said the leader. 'These shots will have been heard. We'll split up. Two cars go home by the Loch Lomond road and the other by Callander. Quick, jump to it! We haven't got much time.'

Rifles and helmets were stowed in the boots along with the corpses, and the cars drove off. The moor returned to quiet and the fox and eagle returned to sleep or to hunting for their own kind.

On a far-off knoll the white stag stood silently, head held high.

Then it, too, set off in the direction of Ben Ledi, a journey that was eventually to save its life.

*   *   *   *

Gavin was happy and excited. He was back in Scotland again to join his friends, the Stewarts, the Clan, for a lengthy summer holiday.

The last time he had come up from London he had joined forces with them in a group they called their Clan Alliance and together they had prevented a gang of thieves from stealing some precious antique silver. It was the most marvellous holiday of his life.

The Clan had taught him how to live out of doors, how to move quietly and secretly in the wild, leaving no traces behind, and because his mother's name had been MacRae and because they had become friends he was allowed to join up with Clare, Michael, and Mot as a fellow Clan member.

He could still remember those days with pleasure, and in his rucksack he had his MacRae clan badge and his tartan sash. He had put his Balmoral hat on his head on the train, much to the amusement of other passengers, but he didn't care. They didn't know the fun and the adventures he had last time.

This time he was going to a farm called Faskally, not far from Callander, where Uncle Fergus and Aunt Elspeth had moved and they had agreed to let the Stewarts and himself stay there during the school holidays. Uncle Fergus was not an uncle of the Stewarts only of himself, but their familes had become such close friends that they all called him Uncle.

'We've plenty of room,' Uncle Fergus had said.

'This place is big and rambling and could do with some more people in it. You can roam the hills and glens and provided you are back here each night and don't get into trouble you'll be left to your own devices.

'There's a small loch nearby with an island and a ruined castle on it and you can go into the hills easily enough. I don't expect we'll be bothered with a gang of crooks again!

'The Stewarts will be here when you arrive and you can stay for all the school holidays if you like.'

Gavin was in ecstasy of anticipation as he left the overnight train at Stirling and boarded an early morning bus which would drop him at the farm road-end. Uncle Fergus had sent him detailed travel instructions, and Clare had included a note-from-the-chief.

He took it from his pocket and read it again. It had a roughly-drawn badge at the top which looked like a unicorn's head, with a motto below it, which said, 'Quidder we'll Sje' (which means 'Whither will Ye?'). Gavin knew it was the badge of one of the Stewart Clans, the Stewarts of Appin, and the motto had a slightly truculent ring about it as if the bearer was saying who-are-you-and-where-are-you-going or why-don't-you-follow-me? Gavin thought it suited the daring Clare.

The note said: 'From the Chief to Gavin. Welcome! When you arrive follow the birch signs through the pinewood to the lochan (she had added "little loch" for him as an explanation). There you will find a birlinn. Take it to the island, but do not leave the shore until you have given your secret sign. Give it once more when you are halfway to the island. Destroy this note and all signs. Signed Clare (The Chief).'

Gavin was puzzled. What on earth was a birlinn? He wasn't sure he would be able to follow the birch signs, and he didn't even know what they were. But, after all, he had outwitted the Clan in a friendly game last time they had met and this had meant he was accepted into the Clan Alliance, so even though he was a city boy he should be able to follow the trail.

He memorised all this and then tore the note into little pieces, to be disposed of carefully later. His aunt was amused because they had barely greeted one another and Gavin had been shown to his room when he told her he was eager to be out and find his friends.

'I know where they are,' said Aunt Elspeth. 'They're on the island. But just you sit down and have something to eat. You've the whole day ahead of you and they can wait.'

Impatiently, Gavin ate. He had dumped his rucksack in his bedroom, had a quick look out of the window and was delighted to see that the steep slopes of a rocky hillside lay just behind his bedroom window, and he lay on the floor trying to follow them out of sight before the line of the roof cut them off. He liked the look of the farm, its strong grey-stone buildings sturdily sited at the top of a little slope, and partially fringed by a grove of ash-trees. The two-storey farmhouse and its outhouses looked as if they so belonged there that they had taken root.

Then, on with his boots and anorak, and out of the door he went heading for the pine wood his aunt had pointed out to him about a quarter-of-a-mile from the house.

Then he stopped. His aunt was still at the door watching him depart. 'Aunt,' he shouted. 'What's a birlinn?'

'It's a boat,' she called. 'It's the old Gaelic name for a small galley.'

A boat! Great! He hurried down the tiny track from the farm gate, across a field besprinkled with rushes, and vanished in the trees.

*   *   *   *

When Gavin got in among the pines he stopped for a few minutes. He tried to recall what Michael and Mot had said to him when he had been on the Ochil Hills the last time he was in Scotland. Take your time to think properly and plan, otherwise you can get into difficulties in the outdoors. That was it. So he sat down, and pulled out the Ordnance Survey map he had brought with him.

He had realised before that maps were great fun and on his last holiday had been able to turn the colours and whorls and insignia into fact, by exploring the hills and woods they had shown. He had also spent a lot of his time in London learning how to map-read and had joined an orienteering club.

It wasn't the same running or walking round a London park as being in Scottish hills but it was great practice and he had become inwardly proud of his ability to navigate, using his compass.

He also took time to check his gear. He was only going to the island, but nevertheless in his rucksack as well as his map, compass and cagoule, he had packed his birdbook, a notebook and pencil, a small pair of binoculars and his trusted gully-knife, a hefty thing with two blades, a tin-opener and a spike.

He sat down on some pine needles and felt the summer sun pleasantly warm through the branches. There was a delicious, fresh scent from the trees, a smell he was to recall again and again in future years.

He leaned against one of the rough trunks and admired their strength and great height, the rough bark, and the way they swept up with their green canopy on the top branches.

Over the winter he had read a little about the Scottish Clans and he knew that the pine tree was the badge of the Clan MacGregor, which had been greatly persecuted in past centuries, and he thought that was a very fitting badge for them — strong, tough and able to withstand great storms.

So, keeping an eye open for any birds which might be in the topmost branches, he opened his map and tried to recall what Aunt Elspeth had said.

'You go across the field to that pine wood,' she had told him. 'You will find a little path running through it and you come to an old wall with a stile. The main road sweeps round there and you will have to cross it. There won't be much traffic but keep a good look out.

'On the other side of the road is another wall and stile and you cross that and enter a birch wood. A tiny track splits into two or three other tracks but Clare told me they have marked the one you have to follow down to the shore. Then you'll see the island. Have fun, but be careful!'

Gavin examined the map and saw Faskally Farm marked, then the wood, the sharp bend of the road, then the wood on the other side and finally the small loch with the island with the word 'Castle' on it beside a Gaelic name, Lochan an Caisteal, which puzzled him.

Then his eye drifted away into wild, wild ground, an

immense area of wood, moors and hills, a mass of brown contour lines, blue burns, and swelling peaks, and strange names, Ben Vorlich, Stuc a' Chroin, Cruach Ardrain, Ben Each, Ben Ledi, Ben Venue, and lonely hill passes and lochs. 'Great!' he muttered to himself. 'What a country!'

A quick check with his compass showed the woodland path running in the direction he wanted to go and off he set, trotting through the trees until he came to an old wall, built of stones, with no cement or mortar, each stone skilfully built on to the other. He knew that in Scotland such walls were called dry-stane dykes.

He quickly hopped over a somewhat rickety wooden stile made of old logs and found himself looking down a steep grassy bank to the road.

He jumped down in a little flurry of dirt and old twigs and when he stepped on to the tarmac he found himself on the edge of a bend and of a kind of lay-by where vehicles could pull in and, indeed, there was an estate-type car there at the moment with three men gathered round it.

As Gavin looked, he could see the car was jacked up and they were obviously changing a wheel after a puncture.

Gavin was partly hidden from the men by tall grasses and scrub bushes which covered the embankment and reached right to the roadside and for a moment or two they did not see him. He was about to step out and cross the road when something about the men's behaviour struck him as odd: they seemed to be getting very bad-tempered.

'Get a move on,' one said angrily.

'I'm being as quick as I can', snapped another. 'The

nuts are stiff. But we're just about there, now.'

He finished tightening the nuts on the wheel and, as Gavin watched, he lowered the car to the ground, removed the jack and, instead of putting it in the boot of the car as Gavin expected, he wrapped it in a cloth and put it on the floor of the seat beside the driver.

Then he turned and saw Gavin. He nudged the others. 'What do you want?' he said truculently.

'Nothing,' said Gavin, taken aback at the tone.

'Well, buzz off,' the man added.

Angry, Gavin crossed the road to the other stile, climbed it and dropped down out of sight over the other dry-stane wall. He remembered the Clan's tuition from last time: keep very still and the chances are you will not be seen. What an odd bunch, and so bad-tempered, he thought. Then he crept close to the wall and peered through a crack.

The men were still talking angrily. They seemed like estate or forestry workers with wellington boots and old jackets. 'There was no need to talk to the kid like that,' said one. 'There's no need to put anyone's back up. That's the way talk starts.'

'Ach, he's only a kid,' said the other. 'I'm getting fed up. We should have been home and off the road hours ago.'

They got back into the car, but just as they did so Gavin heard one of them say: 'Well, it was a good night and a good haul and we had no trouble.'

The aggressive one added: 'No spooky white stag this time.'

The rest laughed. They got in, banged the doors and were off. Gavin raised his head, and peered after them. Good riddance!

Then he saw some dark stains on the tarmac of the lay-by where the car had been.

'They've got an oil leak,' he thought. He decided to go and have a look, although he couldn't quite understand why he did so. Later he was to put it down to the fact that the Clan's skill in the wild helped prod one into examining anything different or odd.

He crossed the stile and went over to the lay-by, feeling he was wasting time when he should have been hurrying on to his rendezvous with the Clan.

He bent down and touched the dark, sticky patch. It wasn't oil. Yet it was clearly fresh and had come from the car. What on earth was it? He lifted his hand and closely examined his fingers. Then, with a shock, he realised what the substance was. Blood!

*   *   *   *

Gavin leaped back over the dyke in a great state of excitement. He was sure it was blood yet the vehicles were certainly not butchers' vans and there was too much blood on the road to come from a cut in a leg or a finger, but then again, perhaps he was being foolish.

'Perhaps it isn't blood after all,' he thought, stopping for a second or two beside the wall and examining the now dried brown stains on the tips of his fingers. 'I suppose it could be anything. Old paint, or farm liquid of one kind or another, something like that.'

He examined his fingers closely. The more he looked, the more the stain looked less and less like blood. His excitement ebbed and he began to remember what he was really here for. Perhaps there was a natural explanation for it all.

It was pleasant in the birchwood. The grass was long and rich with flowers, the sun shone strongly through the leaves making everything a dappled yellow and green and little flickers of wind made the leaves move and shimmer.

Another lesson the Clan had taught Gavin was to stop and look around in the wild: that way you saw interesting things that you never noticed if you were hurrying on or driving around in a car all the time.

His eye caught the silver bark of the birches in the sunlight and he halted to examine the trunks. It was not as smooth as he thought, but most of it was a silver white and he began to see what a lovely tree the birch was. He never saw one in future, in a city garden or park, but he would think of these moments standing silently in a Highland wood, on the verge of a dramatic adventure.

His eye caught a small movement and, as he watched, a tiny brown bird worked its way round the side of the trunk of one of the birches, pecking busily at cracks in the bark. It seemed to be able to glue itself to the side of the tree, working round and round. Then it flew over to another and began the same process again, sometimes hidden from Gavin by the trunk, sometimes with its back to him.

He was learning fast about being hidden in the wild. He stood stock still and the bird ignored him. He couldn't remember what kind of bird it was, a nuthatch perhaps, and then he remembered that he had a task ahead of him and he would have to get a move on. He slipped his rucksack off his shoulders and the bird quickly darted away into the wood. He took out his bird book and thumbed through the illustrations until he found the bird he wanted: a tree-creeper. That was it! It was the first tree-creeper he had seen so he wrote the name and date in his little notebook and then, not before time, he began to think of the Clan again.

Clare's note had said he should look out for signs the minute he crossed the dyke and he examined the faint track that ran through the trees. Sure enough, there was a tiny arrow on the path made out of twigs. If he hadn't been specially looking for it he would have missed it, because the ground was thick with dead twigs and branches lying among the long grasses.

He followed the direction of the arrow and then he found another and, some distance further on, yet another. He had to keep looking at the ground and he began to find that faintly irritating and he wondered why Clare had simply not cut a 'blaze', a prominent cut in the bark of trees, and then he remembered that the Clan's golden rule was that no traces should be left.

He went back to the first sign and threw it away and did the same with the others and then returned until the tiny track wound its way to the top of a little mound and there, through the trees, he could see the glimmering waters of the lochan.

He was just about to dart through and rush down to the shore when he remembered that the Clan would be watching out for him and he wanted to make a good impression. So he slipped very quietly forward to the edge of the trees and closely examined the lochan.

It was about half-a-mile long and a quarter-of-a-mile wide and lay in a little hollow in the hills, fringed right along one end by his birchwood. On the far side and at each end the hills rose, firstly in gentle slopes of rolling moorland, and then swept upwards into steep, boulder-strewn mountains, broken up by cliffs and bluffs and large patches of small broken stones which Gavin knew were called scree and which could be very dangerous for walking on because the stones moved and often tumbled downhill, taking the walker with them or striking people below.

The far side of the lochan was fringed with more birches and with darker-coloured alders, and there were wide reed beds, but it was the small island in the middle that caught his eye. It was only a couple of hundred yards long and also had trees on it, birches, alders, hazels and rowans, and he could make out the walls of a ruined castle, broken and grey, but undeniably walls, with what looked like the remains of a tower at one end. But of the Clan there was no sign.

The island was about three-quarters' way across the lochan and the waters were blue and peaceful in the sun. There was not a sound but the slight stirring of the birches and the soft lap of tiny waves on the shore and there was no movement except the lazy flapping flight of a heron which had been fishing at the edge until Gavin appeared. The heron flew slowly towards the island and Gavin watched it closely to see if it would alter its flight as it passed over the castle, a sign that the Clan were there. He knew from his Ochils' adventure that disturbed birds were often a sure sign of human presence. In forest or hill places the flights of birds could tell you a lot.

The heron kept straight on. Gavin was puzzled. Where were they?

But he knew Clare's firmness as a leader and chief and her note was quite clear. His instructions were to go to the island. He examined the ground again and another arrow-sign took him to the shore and there, moored among some reeds and rocks and quite hidden unless you knew exactly where to look, was a small raft.

Gavin examined it dubiously. 'It looks very small to carry me,' he thought. 'I've never been on such a thing before. But I suppose if the Clan use it, I can use it.'

It was made of long logs with several cross pieces nailing it together and a kind of platform with an edge on top. Gavin stepped on to it gingerly, and the water bubbled up between the logs but the platform and edge stayed dry. He rocked it a little and it was quite stable. A long wooden paddle which looked as if it had come from a proper canoe lay across the platform.

Gavin sat down on a stone and thought about it. He reckoned that you half-crouched using the paddle as if you were in a canoe and didn't try to use it like a punt pole or to wiggle it over the stern.

He got on to the platform and with the boat still anchored, experimented in balancing himself and using the paddle on either side. It seemed all right, but it also seemed a very small raft. The Clan called it a birlinn, so he decided to call it that as well.

He was just about to set off when he remembered that he was supposed to give his call sign before he left the shore and also when he was halfway over.

Each member of the Clan had a call or whistle, the sound of some animal or bird, so that they could link up with one another in the wild but no one else would know they were there. It was also their tracking sign and their signature. They drew their bird or animal on letters or notes or marked it out with a stick in mud or sand.

Gavin recalled that Michael had a tawny owl as his

sign; Mot had a curlew for the hills and a blackbird for the woods. Clare had a thrush in woodland and a lapwing (or peewit) elsewhere, if the terrain suited.

When Gavin had been admitted to the Clan Alliance during his last holiday he had, as part of the welcoming celebrations, decided to make the wood pigeon and the peregrine falcon his signs and calls.

'Well, here goes,' he thought. He had driven his mother into a near-frenzy by going round the house making wood-pigeon calls, and peregrine calls, and trying out a few others as well. He wasn't bad at the pigeon, getting his tongue round the throaty roo-roo sound. His mother had bought him a B.B.C. record of bird-calls and he had spent hours listening to the sounds and perfecting them.

He wondered if it would reach to the island. It seemed very far away. But then, the scene was a peaceful one so he supposed Clare knew what she was doing.

He began to make roo-roo noises, gradually increasing the volume until he was sure it could be heard over a long distance or as long as he could make it without going hoarse or bursting.

He paused, gasping for breath. 'Well, that will have to do,' he said to himself. 'All aboard!'

He stepped on to the platform, stowed his rucksack at his feet, untied the rope from a tree, and tried to paddle away. The birlinn stuck. The water was too shallow, and his weight pressed it down.

Then Gavin got the idea. He tugged the birlinn round until it was in deeper water opposite a large boulder and stepped off the stone on to it and pushed away in one motion. The birlinn rocked precariously, but he was away. He soon got the hang of it, squatting down and sending the raft swishing forward. He found it would go off to the right and left after a few strokes so he began to get the trick of three strokes on either side and the birlinn began to head steadily across the lochan.

Gavin was enjoying himself. He stopped paddling for a few seconds and looked around. The shore seemed quite a long way away but he couldn't see anything except the birchwood and the green hillsides beyond. The water was both dark and clear, which puzzled him. It seemed very pure and it certainly was cold, as he found when he dipped his hand in, but deep down it was a kind of brown and he couldn't tell what depth it was.

A fresh, clean smell came from it and he paddled happily on. The island and the grey walls of the castle got nearer and nearer.

'It's time I gave my second set of calls,' he said to himself, and again the crooning roo-roo went softly across the water.

But the island stayed silent and mysterious.

'Ah, well,' thought Gavin. 'I've done my bit. If they're not there I can always explore the island and meet them at the house at night.'

He paddled on and eventually his birlinn bumped rocks on the shores of the island. He didn't know at this time there was a little inlet on the far side which made a natural harbour and he didn't think of paddling round the island: he was just too relieved to get there.

He got his feet wet jumping ashore, but no matter. He made sure the birlinn was firmly pulled up on to the shore and tied to a tree and the paddle safely stowed, before he put his rucksack on again and set off into the trees to find the castle.

It seemed a very lonely island. 'No one can come here very much,' mused Gavin, who was learning fast. The ground was thick with fallen twigs and branches and undergrowth and it looked like one of these school illustrations of primeval forest.

He had landed quite near the castle but the trees and undergrowth were so thick that he couldn't see it, but he knew it was along to his right. Then he found a tiny track and made better speed until he emerged in a clearing and there, right ahead of him, was a little patch of smooth grass and rising from it a large, high, grey stone wall about twice his height, with little windows cut out in it as though for use by archers or musketmen. It looked very old, and seemed to smack of daring deeds, of fierce men in tartan plaids carrying pistols and swords and sallying forth to war.

Gavin walked round by the wall and found that the tower swelled out in a curve and was several feet above the height of the rest of the wall. It had no windows but he found an entrance like a house door.

It was flanked by stone pillars and was quite low. Gavin began to think that people long ago were very small, but he was wrong. The doorway was small so that anyone entering had to stoop and in past times would have found it difficult to wield a sword, thus giving the defenders an advantage.

There was no door, just a gap and he went into a kind of courtyard, partly covered in flat stones and partly in long grass. A large fireplace stood at one end and Gavin examined it. There were ashes in it, so someone had had a fire here and perhaps not too long ago.

Above the fireplace was a carved coat-of-arms. He could just make out the line of a shield but the rest was too weathered to see it clearly.

The roof had long since gone but little openings led off the courtyard to what looked like other rooms and to the tower. The remains of an old staircase ran up one wall, carved stone steps which ended abruptly at the line of the wall.

Everything was very silent and it seemed to Gavin he had stepped back several centuries in coming to this lonely island and its quiet castle.

He returned to the central courtyard and looked around again.

Then, without warning, a huge spear hurtled through the air and lodged with a swish and a crash in the ground at his feet.

CHAPTER 2

Deer on the Hills

Gavin leapt back in fright for a second, then quickly looked all around. There was nothing to be seen but the grey walls.

He picked up the spear and examined it quickly. Now that he looked at it, it wasn't really a spear at all but a kind of stave or staff, rather like the ones carried by Robin Hood's men in films, and it was intricately carved and painted.

Little loops and whorls had been cut in the bark and then painted in green and yellow and blue until it looked something like these marvellous, intricate, twisting designs that Gavin remembered seeing in photographs of Pictish carved stones and the initial, capital letters at the start of old Celtic documents.

The staff wasn't as good as that, of course, just simple loops and whorls but whoever had decorated it, had done it with sufficient skill to put that idea into Gavin's head.

Old knot-holes down the sides, where twigs or small branches had once grown, had been smoothed down and little pictures of birds and animals painted on them in silhouette. The end of the pole, the point which had struck into the ground, was not very sharp, just rounded off, and Gavin realised it had only stuck in, and not skidded, because the grass in the courtyard was soft.

With one eye on the walls and the doorway and the other on the staff he examined its top. It was roughly carved into the shape of a bird's head, graceful, with a sweep to the neck, and a thin beak and a little crest on top. Instantly a picture from a bird book sprang into Gavin's mind. It was a peewit, also called a lapwing or green plover, and that was Clare's sign.

Gavin chuckled. 'All right, Clare!' he called. 'Come out!'

Three grinning heads emerged at the top of the tower and peered down at him.

'Welcome back,' said Clare, clambering on to the edge of one wall and scrambling down to the line of the main wall before jumping down. Michael and Mot followed her until all three stood in front of Gavin, smiling somewhat self-consciously.

'Hallo,' he said. 'It's great seeing you again.'

'But you didn't see us,' said Clare. 'And we saw you coming over.'

They all laughed and the ice was broken and it was as if they were all back in the Ochils again.

They were all clad alike — old khaki shirts open at the neck, old jeans or other trousers, and trainers on their feet — and they looked tanned and slightly grimy.

'We've been clearing out the den,' said Clare. 'We needed a base like the cave on Dumyat and this place seems good. But it's a mess. The roof fell in years ago and it is all rubble and old rubbish and nettles. But we're getting there.

'It'll make a great Clan base. And we've found some stuff from long ago. Look!'

She held out her hand and in it was a tiny piece of what looked like a metal chain, with finely worked links which were black with age but which looked shiny underneath, and a long, barbed piece of metal which looked as if it might be the end of a spear.

'What is it?' asked Gavin.

'No idea,' said Michael. 'But we'll ask Uncle Fergus when we get back. He'll know.'

Mot chimed in: 'The pointed metal thing might be a spear for catching fish. It's a possibility anyway.'

Gavin looked around. 'Who lived here?' he asked. 'How long has it been like this?'

Clare sat down on a rock and said in the formal manner of one about to recite a great saga: 'The Campbell Clan once had a chief who built seven castles, or took some of them from his enemies and improved them, and they all guarded his lands. This was one of them and it was captured by the MacDonalds and others when they were at war centuries ago and when the Campbells took it back later it went on fire and the roof fell in.

'It has been like that ever since. The people who had the farm before Uncle Fergus didn't bother too much about it and just left it as it is and because it can't be seen from the road hardly anyone comes over here.

'It's called Lochan an Caisteal. You'd better get your notebook out, Gavin, because the name is a Gaelic one.'

She spelled it out and told Gavin it was pronounced Lochan an Hascheel, and meant the-small-loch-of-the-castle.

'Gaelic names are interesting,' she added as an after-thought, 'and if you are navigating on the hills the meaning of the hill names can tell you a lot about the ground, like the mossy peak, the sharp ridge, the stony place, or the people who once lived there.'

Gavin thought about this for a moment and made a note.

Then he remembered the name of the farm, Faskally. 'What does that mean?', he asked.

'It's a mix-up into English of some Gaelic words meaning rest-in-the-woods,' said Clare.

'It's rather a nice name but not much good to us because we've work to do.'

Michael laughed. 'Come on,' he said. 'The chief calls! Follow me, Gavin, and I'll show you what we're doing.'

He led the way through a doorway leading off the courtyard and Gavin found himself in a room with enough space to let four or five people lie down and still have some room to spare. The floor was of battered earth.

Long branches and poles had been laid across the roof which was open to the sky.

'That's what we're doing,' said Mot. 'It's the best room in the place. It's sheltered and mostly dry and the line of the walls hides it from the farm shore and from the hillside, and it is fairly well screened by the trees. If we can put a decent roof on we can leave stuff here or shelter in rain.'

Gavin asked: 'Where do you cook?'

Michael replied: 'We use the old fireplace mainly but the island is small and we don't like taking too much wood here. You don't often see a wood which has lain so undisturbed over the years and we wanted to leave it that way. So each time we come over we tow a raft of logs and branches and stack them in another of the rooms and they dry out there.'

Sure enough, when Gavin peeped round a corner into another recess it was about half-full of old, dead branches.

Mot added: 'But we don't cook too much here on an open fire because the smoke can be seen and we don't want people to know about our den. The loch is only deep in places. We've got a stove from a camping shop and we leave that here in a waterproof bag and use that quite a lot.'

Gavin looked around and said, 'It seems pretty heavy. Won't some of the stonework come down on us?'

Clare replied: 'No, the previous farm owner had ideas about excavating the whole thing and he repaired some of the walls before he started on that, but for some reason he never got round to his researches after he finished fixing up the dangerous bits of the walls. But let's get to work. Dump your stuff, Gavin, and we'll get on with the roof.'

So Gavin took his rucksack off and his anorak and rolled up his sleeves.

'Lead me to it,' he said, laughing.

Clare, Michael and Mot took him round the side of the castle wall to where a pile of long branches, neatly trimmed, were stacked. Clare produced a pile of old rope. 'We got this at the farm,' she said. 'It's old and they didn't need it. We have to make the roof sloping so that the water will drip off, but that's all right because the inner wall is higher than the outer.'

Gavin watched as Mot climbed up and began to clear old stones and rubble from along the line of the inner wall and to tug some poles across the gap and jam them into place.

Michael climbed up the other wall and adjusted them. When six or seven were in place Clare cut a notch in them at each end and then cut off several lengths of rope.

'We need to weight them down,' she told Gavin. 'Otherwise a strong wind could take the whole roof off.'

She picked up a stone about the size of a large, thick book and said to Gavin, 'Hunt around and find me about six or seven of those.'

Gavin scrabbled around on the ground, glad to be part of the Alliance again, and quickly produced them.

Clare tied the rope on to them, running it crosswise each way so the stone was securely held as if in a kind of loose basket. Then she handed up the other end of the rope to Mot, who tied it round the notch in the pole. Then she slowly lowered the stone almost to the ground until the rope was taut, and let it go.

In no time at all it seemed the poles were securely anchored to the inner wall, first by being lodged in niches in the wall above and, secondly because the weight of the hanging stones kept them firmly in place.

Michael and Gavin did the same to the ends of the poles hanging over the outer wall until there were eight pieces of dangling rope at each end with the stones a few inches from the ground. A basic roof structure was secure.

'Fine,' said Clare. 'But we need at least eight cross-pieces. Gavin, would you find eight branches about two inches thick and trim them with your knife and then give them to Michael and Mot. But they must be long enough to cross the roof and a bit more after that.'

Gavin hunted among the poles and gladly whipped out his knife and did a bit of trimming of old twigs and knobbly bits until he found what he wanted.

He handed them up and Michael laid them crossways over the weighted poles and then marked them with a pencil where they touched the others. He handed the poles to Mot who cut a shallow notch in each and they were then turned over and laid securely back in place, the notch keeping them firm against the long weighted poles.

'That's not bad,' said Clare. 'Not bad at all. But we need to lash them securely together.'

Gavin stood back and watched for a bit, glad of the rest after all that pole-cutting and stone-hauling and, not for the first time, he admired the efficient, practical way Clare tackled things.

She cut more rope into sections and then she and the boys securely lashed each cross piece to the longer poles, winding the rope skilfully backwards and forwards, tightly and securely, until she tied the final knots.

'Try that, Gavin,' she said. Gavin clambered up on to the outer wall and took hold of one of the poles. He gave it a gentle shake.

'Harder, man,' said Clare. 'Give it a good tug.'

Gavin took hold with both hands and pulled. The poles stayed securely in place.

'All right,' said Clare. 'That'll do for today. We'll have a break and then we'd better get back to the farm before they start fussing. But tomorrow we'll come back and get on with the roof. We'll have a fire today as it is Gavin's first day.'

They all moved back into the courtyard and gathered

round the old, stone fireplace.

Clare continued to give orders. 'Michael, you get the food and plates out. Mot, you get some larger wood. Gavin, let's see if you still have your old skill. You can light the fire!'

Gavin gulped a little. It had been a long time. He cast his mind back to what he had been told and what he had done in their Ochils adventure. First of all, safety had to be thought about. Well, he was nowhere near dry woods or moorland, so there was no danger of starting fires. There had been rain in the night and the island grass and trees were still wet here and there, and he was cooking in a proper fireplace so there was no danger of his fire spreading; nor need he take precautions against leaving an ugly mess by digging out turf for his fire and then replacing it.

'This is going to be easy,' he thought. 'All I need is very dry kindling.' While Clare watched him with amusement, he raked around in crannies in the castle, and in sheltered corners, until he had collected a little pile of bone-dry, very thin twigs, dead bracken and tiny slivers of bark. Then he took a larger piece shaped like a 'Y', stuck it in the middle of the fireplace and put his kindling round it.

He built a pile of larger twigs beside him, being careful to take them from dead branches on trees and not from the ground, where there is always damp. These damper ones would do once he had got the fire going.

Meanwhile, Michael spread out a green groundsheet. Mot put out mugs and plates, some apples and biscuits, and little jars which contained tea and sugar, and a bottle which contained milk.

He also produced a tiny, light kettle which Gavin

decided was an advance on an open dixie with a tea bag hanging in it.

Clare handed Gavin a box of matches and said with a grin, 'Only two, mind.'

Gavin checked to see if there was any wind which might blow his match out and then lit the first one and quickly applied it to a little opening he had made in his small pile of dry kindling. Some dry bracken flared up and began to lick the others. Then it dwindled and went out.

'Curses,' muttered Gavin. Then he lit the second and put it further into the middle. Again the wood flared up and as the flames spread to other bits Gavin blew gently and soon his whole wigwam of tiny twigs, slivers of bark and old bracken was well alight.

A cheer came from the others. Elated, he piled on more dry wood and only when the fire was well alight did he add some larger pieces. Clare pushed a couple of large blackened stones closer to each side of the blaze and then carefully placed the kettle on the larger wood. Flames curled round it, and they all settled down.

Gavin happily chewed an apple as he watched Clare pop a couple of tea bags inside the little kettle and, a few minutes later, lift it off by a loop attached to it, using a long, forked stick which was kept at the side of the fire-place.

She poured the tea and they lay comfortably around and ate more biscuits.

'Well, it's good seeing you, Gavin,' Clare said.

'And it's very good seeing you,' said Gavin, confining his remarks to that as he felt any further show of emotion would be embarrassing.

'What a super stick,' he then said, picking up the

spear from the ground and handing it to Clare. 'You didn't half make me jump.'

'It wasn't really fair,' replied Clare. 'We asked you to make your pigeon call when you were leaving the shore and when you were halfway over so we knew exactly where you were and where to hide. But you didn't know where we were.'

Gavin examined the stick again. He noticed that the paint was bright and new and the stick had been given what looked like a coat of clear varnish, making it gleam.

'It's not really a stick,' said Clare. 'It's a stave. We've all got them. They're for ceremonial parades.'

Gavin knew of Clare's liking for solemn ceremonies so he simply asked where she had got it.

'She made it,' chimed in Michael. 'We've all got them,' added Mot. 'The best ones are made of ash or hazel, but they've got to be cut before the sap rises. Uncle Fergus cut them some time ago and gave them to us.'

'It's easily done,' said Clare. 'Once you've got a decent stick, you just trim any small twigs off it and then decide what your designs are going to be. Any sharp knife will do, but you have got to ensure you leave most of the bark in place. Then you paint your designs with a small brush or a pen into the spaces you've cut in the bark. After that you can give the whole thing a coat of clear varnish and that protects the colours and makes it look even better.'

Gavin examined it again. The peewit's head was very well carved. 'How did you do that?' he asked.

'That was a bit of luck,' said Clare. 'There was a join to another branch there and it lent itself to being carved like a head. I drew the outline of a head on paper, then marked it on the wood in chalk and then used a small saw. Uncle Fergus gave me a hand because it was a bit tricky.'

Gavin was enchanted with the idea. 'Where's yours?' he asked Michael.

'Mot and I left ours at the farm,' he said. 'We try and take care of them as they might mark easily, being so carved and painted, but Clare wanted to take hers to show you on your first day.'

Gavin handed the stave back to Clare and made up his mind that, before the holiday was out he, too, would have one like the Clan's, painted and varnished, a cross between an ancient Celtic carving and an Indian totem pole.

'How long have you got for holidays?' asked Mot. 'A fortnight, same as us?'

'That's right,' said Gavin. 'But we can do a lot in a fortnight.'

'We sure can!' said Clare. 'One thing we've planned is to go up Ben Buidhe* and spend the night out and watch the sun coming up. Uncle Fergus and Aunt Elspeth say we can go provided the forecast is for a dry night and they see us off and welcome us back, and check our route.

'It'll be good fun. We've plenty of gear and we'll be pretty sure of seeing deer.'

Deer! Gavin gulped over his tea and choked.

'What on earth's the matter?' said Clare, as Michael and Mot clapped him on the back until he had finished spluttering.

'Deer! Stag! Blood!' gasped Gavin. 'I meant to tell you but I forgot. I saw a lot of odd men beside the road

*pronounced Boo-ee

on the other side of the lochan, the farm side, and they had a puncture and one of them told me to buzz off when they saw me watching them in the lay-by.'

Mot chuckled. 'Lots of grown-ups are like that,' he said.

'No, this was serious,' said Gavin. 'I came through the woods on my way to see you and crossed the dry-stane dyke (he was secretly pleased to get that term right) on to the road. They were gathered round their car. Two cars, now I come to think of it.

'Just before they all got back in and drove away I looked back from behind the dyke on the other side of the road and I heard them talking. And when they had gone there was a big stain on the side of the road. I went across and touched it. And it was blood. Or what looked like blood.'

'You're joking,' said Clare. 'You're having us on!'

'No, honest,' said Gavin. 'It was quite fresh and I touched it. Later I began to think it was maybe motor oil or old paint or something else, but it looked like blood.'

'That's odd,' said Clare, pondering. 'What kind of cars had they, vans or something like that?'

'No,' said Gavin. 'They were estate cars. And there's another thing. When he had finished repairing the puncture and putting the wheel back he put the jack on the floor of the seat beside the driver.'

'Well, that's all right,' said Clare. 'Nothing funny about that. It simply means they had a very full boot or didn't want to spend any time fussing around.'

'But there's something else,' said Gavin. 'One of them said they had had a good night and a good haul, and they had once seen a spooky white stag.'

There was a thunderstruck silence.

Clare sat bolt upright. Michael and Mot, like one man, put their mugs down together, their faces alert with attention.

'Are you sure?' Clare said tautly.

'Why, what's so special about the white stag?' asked Gavin.

Clare paused for breath.

'It will be the White Stag of the Corrie Ba. There's a legend that it is really a ghost and it haunts the Corrie Ba.'

Seeing Gavin looking puzzled, she added: 'A corrie is a big hollow in the hills. It's from a Gaelic word meaning bowl-shaped and the Corrie Ba is reputed to be one of the biggest corries in Scotland.

'Some people say the stag is only a tale, a legend. Others say it is real. Uncle Fergus had a man at the door asking about it recently. He said he was writing a book about animals like the Loch Ness Monster, but Uncle Fergus was a bit suspicious of him. He was clearly very rich. He drove a very expensive car with a chauffeur and was well-dressed. Uncle Fergus told him we had no information, but he said he would be around the area for a time and might come back.'

'Well, he wasn't one of the men I saw,' said Gavin. 'They all looked as if they had been hard at work — old clothes, jackets, trousers and wellies.'

Suddenly, Clare thumped one hand into another with a smack that made them all jump.

'I've got it,' she said. 'They've been poaching. They had dead deer in the back. That's where the blood came from.'

Seeing Gavin again looking puzzled she said: 'They

come out in gangs and turn their car headlights on to deer grazing beside the road and, when their lights dazzle the deer, they fire at them. They don't worry if they wound any of them, they just fire into the herd. Some of the deer are wounded and escape and linger for days. It's big business because they can get a lot of money for the meat.

'I hate them. They are cruel men who don't care about any suffering they cause the deer. They're hard to catch, too. Uncle Fergus was saying that the area hadn't been troubled by poachers for some time because the police caught some and they were heavily fined and jailed and their cars and guns confiscated.'

'They must be back again.'

Michael and Mot looked very grave. 'We'd better tell Uncle Fergus when we get back,' Michael said. 'He can tell the police.'

Mot added: 'It's possible they had the deer legally, but I doubt it. And if the white stag is still around we certainly don't want them to get that.'

There was a chorus of agreement.

Then Clare chuckled and suddenly pointed at the hillside. 'There's some they didn't get! There, on the skyline, about threequarters way up Ben Buidhe.'

Michael and Mot squinted upwards and then said, almost in unison, 'Ah, got them.' Gavin, too, peered upwards and then said, 'I'm sorry I can't see them.'

Clare came over beside him and pointed again: 'Do you see that big cliff?'

Gavin nodded.

'Follow the skyline upwards until you see a prominent dip and bump. Got it?'

Gavin nodded again.

Clare went on: 'Imagine the dip and bump are the middle of a clock. Look where two o'clock would be and you'll see some tiny dots with one or two on the skyline. They're deer.'

Gavin did so, and there against the hillside were some brown specks, slowly moving towards the sky-line and then crossing it. Smashing! The first red deer he had actually seen in the wild.

Then he remembered he had his old bird-watching binoculars in his rucksack.

Hurriedly, he pulled them out and focused them on the deer. There were about twenty in all, he thought, and they were just about all over the skyline.

Then Gavin let out a gasp. 'Clare!' he said, in a great state of excitement.

'One of them's white!'

CHAPTER 3

On Parade

The Clan had a warlike air about them as they hurried down to the shore.

'We've got to report this when we get back,' said Clare. 'Poachers *and* a white stag. We'll have to keep a good look-out for them in future. We can't let them get away with killing deer on our ground and we're certainly not going to let them kill the white stag.'

'Perhaps we could mount hill patrols?' said Mot. 'We could show that we're around and scare them off.'

'Yes, that's a good idea,' added Michael.

Gavin waited silently, as he generally did, on Clare summing the matter up.

'No,' she said. 'We don't want to scare them off. And we don't want to be seen. We want to catch them. Tomorrow we can have a council of war, and we will start with a full ceremonial parade on the island as soon after breakfast as we can get there.

'And we'll finish off the room. We've got to have a decent base.'

She made her way to a thick clump of alders beside the shore and there, hidden by the trees, was a little inlet among the rocks. There, too, was a raft like Gavin's, but longer and larger, with room for three people sitting one in front of the other.

44

'Gosh!' said Gavin. 'How long did it take you to make that?'

'It's been here for ages,' said Clare. 'Uncle Fergus had it in an old barn at the farm and we think it must have been made for children long ago or perhaps for fishing from because there are a lot of trout in the lochan.

'We took it down at the start of the holiday and Uncle Fergus and two of his friends helped us carry it down. It's a bit heavy to paddle but if there are three of us and you don't rock it too much it's not bad. We've even named it.'

Gavin looked at the bow and there, painted in somewhat shaky green letters on the logs, were the words 'The Galley of the Waves.'

'A galley is another Gaelic word for a boat or ship,' said Clare, 'but generally bigger than a birlinn. We made your birlinn ourselves.

'You'd better go and get it, Gavin, and follow us over.'

Gavin had been so full of the conversation that he had forgotten his own birlinn.

'Right!' he said. 'Just before you go, Clare, it occurred to me that someone might be able to swim over to our island. Is the lochan very deep?'

'No,' said Clare. 'It's a problem because the water is only three or four feet deep, but there are deep sections. In fact, if it had been deep all over we wouldn't have been allowed to go on the birlinn or the galley without wearing life-jackets. In the summer people have swum here if they have been on holiday at the farm and the water mainly doesn't go above your chest. But the bottom is very soft and care is needed.

'You've got to be careful about swimming in Scottish lochs because much of the ground falls away in shelves. The water can be warm at the side and then the bottom falls away, the water becomes very cold and even although the day might be very warm the cold gives people cramp and they drown.

'That's something for your notebook, Gavin. But our lochan is all right.'

Gavin dutifully pulled out his notebook and wrote down 'take care about swimming in lochs'.

Then he sped off to get his birlinn, hopped on board and paddled out into the loch. He found it much easier this time.

Ahead of him he could see the galley bashing through the water, the three paddles making it send up a long bow wave and wake which eventually floated back to Gavin's birlinn making it rock when it caught him.

Both rafts landed safely.

'Now pull them well up,' said Clare. 'Gavin, we've got a hidden place for the galley. Put the birlinn back where you found it in these bushes.'

Michael, Mot and Clare tugged the galley over the stones and into the trees, where they rolled it into a little hollow among the birches and then covered it with old branches and torn up ferns. It could not now be seen by any casual passer-by.

'What's your hiding place like, Gavin?' said Clare coming over to inspect. Gavin had tugged the birlinn in among the rocks and it was well screened by bushes.

'That's fine,' said Clare.

'Michael, have you got those two historical finds to show Uncle Fergus?'

Michael tapped his small rucksack and then, having second thoughts, opened it and looked in. He held out the small interwoven chain and the metal spear-head. 'Both safe,' he said.

'Let's go and eat,' said Clare.'We've got a lot of planning to do.'

Just before they left the shore, they turned and scanned the skyline of the hills behind the lochan, but the deer had gone.

Gavin thought the hills looked magnificent. Seamed and rough, steep and rocky, the sun lit up all the little hollows and crags, making them yellow and golden, turning to black when the beams moved on.

'What a great place to go,' he said, pointing to the hills.

'But we are going to go there,' said Clare.'That's the way we'll take when we go up Ben Buidhe to see the sun coming up. It'll be fun all right. Now let's get back to the house. Tomorrow we go to war!'

Michael and Mot both let out a kind of war-whoop. 'Creag-an-Sgairbh!' they shouted.

Gavin laughed. 'What on earth does that mean?' he asked.

'It's the war-cry of the Stewarts of Appin,' said Clare. 'It means "The Cormorant's Rock". Actually, we're a long way from the area called Appin but we do see cormorants on the lochs from time to time so we've adopted that as our slogan. It's pronounced Crek-ahn-Sgarv.'

She spelled it out for Gavin who wrote it in his notebook.

'Creag-an-Sgairbh!' he shouted.

'Creag-an-Sgairbh!' echoed Clare, Michael and

Mot, and the ancient slogan resounded up the hillsides
as it had done in past centuries, a clarion call to war.

*   *   *   *

'The white stag is absolutely fascinating,' said Uncle
Fergus, when he was told what Gavin had seen and
heard. 'There are all kinds of tales about it but it hasn't
been seen for years. Most people thought it was just a
story and that it had been confused with an old legend
from the time of James VI.

'But I'll tell the local police and we'll keep an eye out
for the men. If you think you see the same vehicles
again, Gavin, take the numbers and we can check up on
them. And if you see the stag again, please tell us
instantly.'

'Right!' said Gavin. The white stag fascinated him
too. 'What exactly went on when James VI was King?'
he asked.

Uncle Fergus told them that when James VI of Scotland had also become King of England at the Union of
the Crowns between Scotland and England in 1603, it
had been reported to the King in London that a white
deer had been seen in the Corrie Ba, in the Blackmount
Hills, near Glen Coe.

'The King's forester from Windsor came up here one winter and he found it very tough going, poor man, because the conditions were far more wild than he was accustomed to. The local chiefs gave him hospitality because he was from the King and he told them he hoped to capture the white deer. It was a hind, Gavin — that is, a female deer — not a stag like the one you saw.'

'And did they capture it?' asked Gavin.

'No,' said Uncle Fergus. 'The winter was too wild, but they did muster hundreds of men in the hope of driving it into a kind of fold, called an elrig, and capturing it there. So the forester went back to Windsor again, empty-handed.'

Gavin felt glad that the white hind had stayed free. Perhaps it was an ancestor of the stag he had seen.

'Are deer fierce?' he asked.

'Nowadays, when they are hunted by man with guns, they run,' said Uncle Fergus. 'But in past centuries they were driven by men and dogs into the elrigs and there they were killed by arrows or by swords and axes and sometimes a cornered stag would turn and gore hunters.'

Gavin remembered all this the next day when he was on the island. It was to be a full-dress occasion. Slightly self-conscious, he had put on his bonnet with the Mac-Rae badge on it and draped his MacRae tartan sash over his shoulder. Having done that he began to feel a bit better.

It seemed fitting somehow to wear these things in the ruins of a castle, where fierce clansmen had battled for its possession, and the MacRae tartan shone a splendid red in the morning sun.

Michael and Mot were sitting on boulders, also

wearing bonnets but with the Stewart of Appin badge pinned to the front.

They had added a sprig of leaves to their badges and were waiting for Clare, who had been delayed talking to Aunt Elspeth and who had told them to go over in the galley and she would follow on in the birlinn.

Gavin had enjoyed that trip. He had more confidence after the day before and Mot and Michael were very expert. He watched them paddle for a time before joining in, lending his paddle's support first to one and then to the other as the galley forged out into the lochan and headed for the castle, leaving a long, zig-zag wake behind it.

'What's that in your hats?' asked Gavin.

'They're oak-leaves,' said Mot. 'They're the badge of the Stewarts of Appin. Clare said that today was to be full-dress to start with and she'll complain like mad if we don't do as she says.'

Michael added: 'Before the days when tartan took on definite patterns the different Clans used plant badges as lucky charms, oak for Stewarts, ivy for the Gordons, heather for the MacDonalds, bog-myrtle for the Campbells and so on.'

Mot said: 'Clare reads up on all these things and keeps us up to the mark. I forget what the MacRae plant badge is. You don't happen to know, do you, Gavin? If so, I suggest you go and pick some otherwise you'll get a chiefly reprimand!'

Gavin laughed. He knew Clare's reprimands. They were always delivered with a grin and all the boys accepted it in good humour because she was normally proved right in her decisions and in what she wanted them to do.

'I'll find out from Uncle Fergus' library when I get back,' he said. 'Then I'll know for next time. I wonder where she's got to? She's taking a long time to come over.'

Mot said: 'Yes, she is, but Aunt Elspeth and Uncle Fergus wanted to know more about our plans for going up Ben Buidhe to see the sun coming up and as it depends on the weather forecast they didn't want to waste too much time when we actually decide to go. So they were chatting to Clare about it now.'

A friendly silence fell and then Gavin said: 'Would you teach me something about deer and how to watch them?' He had suddenly remembered the tuition given to him in Menstrie wood by Michael which had resulted in his staying hidden from the gang of criminals and which he had used so often since in bird watching.

'Yes, of course,' said Mot. 'What do you want to know?'

'You'd better get that notebook of yours out,' said Michael.

'I suppose I really want to know everything,' said Gavin. 'When do they get their antlers, when are their calves born, how many are here, all that kind of thing?'

'Hold on, hold on,' said Mot. 'One thing at a time!'

'We look like having a bit of a wait before Clare comes over,' said Michael. 'Anyway, she'll signal from the shore and from halfway over and we'll hear her.'

Gavin got out his notebook and pencil and sat poised.

Mot said: 'The red deer is our biggest mammal. There are hundreds on the hills here but you have to move quietly and know where to look to see them. And you have to watch for the wind. If it is blowing from you to them they can smell you and will run. If it is blowing towards you, that is better, but you still have to move very carefully and quietly.'

'And they're shot,' chimed in Michael. 'They're shot for sport in the late summer and autumn.'

Gavin's face fell. Shot! That was dreadful. Michael went on: 'But they are part of the revenue of some estates and the meat, called venison, is sold abroad and the stalking, as it is known, is let to wealthy people.'

Gavin wrote all this down.

'But if there are bullets flying around won't we get hit going on to the hills? he asked.

'No,' said Mot. 'There are dates for stalking, both stags and hinds, and it is against the law to shoot outside these times and many estates won't allow shooting on a Sunday even within these dates.'

'So we stay off many of the hills during the peak of stalking, say mid-August to mid-October, except for the lower glens, and we can always get Uncle Fergus to check if there's shooting going on if we want to go elsewhere within the full dates. But the rest of the time, there's no bother.'

Gavin heaved a sigh of relief. 'So we're all right now,' he said.

'Yes,' the boys chorused. Michael said, 'But it's not long until the start of the season so make the most of it.'

Gavin smiled to himself. He certainly would!

He wrote some more notes and then asked, 'When are the calves born?'

'June, and up on the high ground,' said Mot. 'You can sometimes come across them and if you do, the mother won't be far away so we move on as quickly as possible. She'll get very alarmed.'

Gavin continued to write. Later he would read and re-read his notes until he remembered them.

'What about the antlers?' he asked. He remembered seeing pictures of stags with huge, sweeping antlers and he thought they looked fierce.

He wrote more notes as the boys told him that the deer threw off or 'cast' their antlers in March.

'You can often find them,' said Mot. 'They're just lying around in the heather.'

'But they go a kind of grey-white very quickly as a result of the weather,' said Michael. 'And the deer chew them because they contain salt so they sometimes vanish. Clare made a frame for a home-made rucksack out of a set, and used the horns for the frame. Uncle Fergus helped her use steam to bend them. Her bag was part of an old canvas hold-all and she made holes for a string at the top. The whole thing looks great.'

Mot added: 'And it's very tough, and it's very waterproof, not like some other rucksacks you can get today. But it's big and she only uses it for overnight outings.'

Michael explained that by July the new antlers were well grown and covered in a kind of outer skin, called velvet, which eventually rubbed off.

'And in the autumn they fight,' said Mot.

"Fight?' said Gavin, remembering the elrig story. 'Who with?'

Michael smiled. 'With one another,' he said. 'The stags get a kind of harem of hinds as wives and fight their rivals for them. They roar and charge one another and try and strike one another with their hooves, and have trials by strength with their antlers locked and each pushing like mad.'

'Goodness, I'd like to see that,' said Gavin.

'Yes, it's a great time,' said Michael.

'It's known as the rut,' added Mot.

Both boys went silent for a moment or two, each reflecting on past autumns when the hills and moor were tawny brown and yellow and the angry bellows of the stags echoed in the corries and glens, a magnificent time.

They were sorry Gavin would not be here then to see it. 'They are great to see on the hills,' said Mot.

Gavin agreed. He had only seen the red deer that once, but he was thrilled to have been able to pick them out and watch them drift to the skyline and then over and he would never forget looking through the binoculars and seeing them grow bigger, a mixture of hinds and stags, with proud heads and then, at the rear, but walking with grace and with a lordly air, the white stag with the big antlers.

Like the other boys he fell silent for a few minutes, falling into the outdoor habit of musing or pondering quietly on what he had seen.

The island was very quiet. The trees and grasses were unmoving in the heat and the waters of the lochan were still. There was an occasional croak of a raven high on the hillside, but that was all.

Then over the water came the sound of a thrush making an alarm call, the kind of sound Gavin had heard in spring woods when someone had accidentally strayed too near a nest.

'That's her!' said Mot, springing up.

Michael climbed on to the wall and peered over. 'Here she comes,' he said.

Gavin found a niche in the stones and pulled himself

up. Through the green of the trees he could just make out the blue sheen of the water and then he saw Clare coming over in the birlinn.

He watched her until halfway when she slowed a little and gave another call, this time the kind of song a thrush makes in the evening or very early morning when many birds sing.

It sounded a bit odd. Mot and Michael looked at one another.

'That's not like her,' said Michael.

'No,' said Mot. 'Her timing is a bit out.'

They watched her as she fell to paddling again and soon they could see that she was fairly making the birlinn speed along. Then just before they lost her as she neared the shore, to disappear below the walls as she headed for the landing place, she looked up at the castle walls where she knew they would be. Then she let rip the thrush's alarm call again.

Michael and Mot immediately answered with their signs of the angry chatter of a disturbed blackbird and the sharp kee-wick of the tawny owl and Gavin, not to be outdone, added his pigeon roo-roo a few seconds later. In reply, Clare silently waved her hand round her head in a circular motion, but slowly, deliberately, not in a frenzy. Gavin recalled another golden rule in the wild. Don't make noisy, jerky or sudden movements if you want to be unseen.

Michael and Mot looked quickly at one another. 'It's trouble,' said Mot. 'Something urgent has happened.'

CHAPTER 4

The Men at the Table

Clare burst in through the castle doorway, her rucksack bumping on her back. She had run from the landing place.

'Sorry, boys,' she said. 'The ceremonial parade's postponed! We've got to move quickly. I think I've tracked the men but I don't want to make a fool of myself and I need Gavin's help.

'They're supposed to be at Roddy's shop — the shop is also the post office, Gavin — at midday and it is now after ten. We need to get a good look at them. We're not going to let these thugs get away with it, shooting deer on our hills.

'And they might get the white stag.'

She switched her glance quickly from one to another. 'We'd better get cracking!' she said. 'Put the special gear away.'

'But Clare,' said Michael. 'How do you know all this? How do you know about the men?'

'Yes,' said Mot. 'You've got to tell us all about it. Surely a few minutes more won't matter.'

'Sorry!' said Clare. 'You're quite right. I got a bit carried away and more and more frustrated when I couldn't get away from the house.'

She glanced at her watch.

'Sit down for a quick minute,' she said. 'But it will have to be quick.'

'I was discussing with Aunt Elspeth our night expedition to see the sun coming up and it took longer than I expected. I thought I had time to sprint down to the village shop and get a few things. We need some candles over here, some replacement canisters for the stove and some more string — and Aunt Elspeth asked me to post some letters for her.

'So I ran down there and bought my stuff and Roddy — that's the shop owner, Gavin — was asking how we all were and I was sticking stamps on Aunt Elspeth's letters when I noticed there were four men at a table in that little tea-room place Roddy has at the side.'

She paused for breath. 'Well, go on, go on,' said Mot.

Clare continued: 'I didn't take much notice of them at first. They were busy drinking coffee and lots of people drop in there to do that when they are driving past.'

She paused for a second and then said: 'I've just got a hunch that it might be them, but I've not too much to go on. I thought I heard one of them mention deer but that was all and it was only once.'

Michael looked at her, surprised. 'But that's not much to get steamed up about, Clare. Why are you making such a fuss? Anyone could have said deer. They might have meant Roddy's prices!'

Mot chuckled.

'Yes, come on, Clare,' he said. 'Surely you've got more to tell us.' Clare replied, 'It was just that they all seemed to be wearing the kind of clothing you mentioned, Gavin, and they were rather huddled together.

'People do sometimes talk quietly in cafés, but most of the time they chatter away quite openly. There just seemed something slightly furtive about them.'

She stopped and then said: 'I know it is not much to go on, but I've just got this hunch about them. They *look* like your men, Gavin, and they just seemed slightly quieter and more secretive than other people. It's hard to explain, but I think they should be checked out.'

Gavin looked at her for a moment. Clare was rarely wrong, he knew. She noticed everything that went on and if she felt the men were odd then that was enough for him.

'All right, Clare,' he said. 'Let's have a look.'

Encouraged, Clare went on: 'I concentrated like mad but I couldn't stick stamps on all day. That would make them suspicious. So I dropped the letters on the floor and when I bent to pick them up I had a good look at them.

'Then one of them said to the others that they would meet again there at midday. I began to think they would notice me listening in so I had to go over to Roddy and talk about the weather and our holiday.

'And then they all left. But we've really got to get a move on if we want to be there by midday.'

'Would you recognise them?' said Mot.

'Yes, I think so,' said Gavin. 'One of them told me to buzz off. I'd remember him!'

Michael chuckled.

'We might be wasting our time,' he said. 'But if they were talking about deer, it's worth checking up on them.'

'Yes, I'm certain we should,' said Clare.

'I suggest we get our ceremonial clothing stowed

away. We can go to the shop, take a look at them, and then come back here and finish the den and decide what to do. There's quite a bit of roofing to be done. And, if there's time, we'll have the parade.'

Michael went through to the room which they had partially roofed and pulled out a large, tin chest, painted brown.

'We got this in an old attic and Uncle Fergus said we could have it. It was very difficult bringing it over in the galley but we managed it.'

He opened it up and Gavin saw that it contained large waterproof bags. He watched as Michael and Mot put their tartan sashes, balmorals and badges inside, and then he did the same. The bags were tied at the neck, put back in and the lid closed.

Mot dragged the chest back into the den and covered it with old ferns. Alongside it was an old groundsheet tightly rolled up, which was also covered.

'We've got one or two other boxes there, Gavin,' he said. 'They're watertight, too, and we keep other equipment in them, including the dirk and other things you saw in the Dumyat cave.'

Gavin gave a little shiver of pleasure. He still remembered the Dumyat cave and that moment when he had opened the mysterious chest and out had fallen a tartan roll of cloth and a jewelled dirk within it, an event which led to his first meeting with the clan.

'Will we use it on parade?' he asked.

'Yes,' said Mot. 'Clare wouldn't have anything else!'

'That's enough chattering,' said Clare. 'Let's get going if everything is safely hidden.'

They took a last look around and then headed for the landing inlet.

Michael, Mot and Clare boarded the galley with practised ease and Gavin followed, somewhat more shakily, in the birlinn and they paddled their way back to the shore.

The boats were hidden again and they half-ran, half-walked back to the farm and then down a side road to the village and Roddy's shop-cum-post office.

They made it with about ten minutes to spare.

'Well, what do you lot want?' said Roddy jocularly, who knew the Stewarts and their uncle and aunt well. 'Why are you looking so puffed?'

'We're in rather a hurry today,' said Clare. 'But we thought we might have some juice.'

'Sure,' said Roddy. 'What would you like?'

Clare glanced at the boys. 'Orange,' said Michael. 'Suits me,' added Mot. Gavin nodded. 'Four oranges, please, Roddy,' said Clare, handing over the money.

She led the way into the side-room Roddy used as a tea-room, hissing as she went ('You lot can pay me back later!') and they all sat down, bottles in front of them and heads close together.

Clare leaned forward and whispered: 'Gavin, change places with me so you can watch the other tables. I'll sit with my back to them in case any of them remember me from this morning.'

She and Gavin quietly moved over and they had no sooner done so when the door opened and four men came in and sat down in the opposite corner. They took no notice of the Clan and one of them called to Roddy to bring four coffees.

They began to talk in low voices but what they were saying could not be made out.

'Do you recognise them?' whispered Clare to Gavin.

He shot a quick glance and muttered: 'It's very like them but I can't see the one with his back to me.'

Clare said, 'Go to the door for a minute or ask Roddy something and then come back in and get a good look at him.'

Gavin went through to the main shop and wandered up to the counter and asked Roddy what time he shut on Saturday.

'Teatime, same as every other day except Sunday,' said the mystified Roddy. 'But your friends know that.'

'Sorry, I forgot,' said Gavin and strolled through to the other room, taking a quick look at the man who had previously had his back to him.

He tried to remember the angry face in the lay-by telling him to buzz off, black hair, moustache, about thirty or so, slightly red face. He slowly let his gaze drift away remembering the rule about no jerky movements which attract attention and sat down in his place.

He drank his juice silently.

Clare, Michael and Mot eyed him intently.

'Well,' said Clare. 'Is it him?'

'Yes it is,' said Gavin quietly. 'I'm sure.'

*   *   *   *

The bell on the door of Roddy's shop gave a tinkle as a large man pushed the door open and walked in, looking around as he did so. He ignored Roddy, who waited inquiringly behind his counter, and walked through to the tea-room section and, without hesitating, went up to the group of men and said something to them in a low voice.

He ignored the Clan who sat silently, heads hunched

over their glasses of juice, just like any other group of children on holiday, but who were avidly trying to hear every word.

After a sentence or two, one of the men took a chair from beside a neighbouring table and pulled it over and the large man joined them at their table. Another of the men, the one with the red face who had shouted at Gavin in the lay-by, got up and went through to Roddy and ordered another batch of coffees.

'He looks foreign,' hissed Clare, and Michael, Mot and Gavin all did their best to have a look at him without being too obvious, although Clare had her back to him and only saw him when he first came into the tea-room.

'What's he like?' she said softly. Gavin muttered: 'He looks rich, big coat, smart suit. He's very fat. Like an ogre! We should call him that from now on.'

Michael who could look through the tea-room entrance to the front door added, 'There's a car outside with a chauffeur.'

Clare said excitedly: 'A man with a chauffeur called on Uncle Fergus to ask him if he had heard about a white stag in this area! Do you remember? Uncle Fergus didn't like him and he went away again. He said he was writing a book about odd animals, like the Loch Ness monster.'

'That's right,' said Mot. 'It seems like the same chap. What on earth can he want with that lot?'

The murmur of voices came from the table across the small room but the Clan couldn't make out what was being said.

Clare said: 'We can't sit here for ever, whispering. They'll get suspicious. We've got to have some idea of what they are up to. When he goes out to his car they might continue talking. It's a slim chance, but we're not hearing anything in here.

'Gavin, why don't you and Mot go out, leaving Michael and myself here so that they don't get suspicious. Hide on the far side of the wall beside the car. It's just possible you might hear something. If you don't hear anything then we're not worse off than we are now.'

'Good idea,' said Michael. 'If only two of us go they won't notice anything and Clare and I can sit and talk about our holiday in a way that won't arouse their attention.'

'Sure!' said Gavin. 'I don't mind. It's worth a try. And if Mot and I both go, we can back one another up if need be.'

After a few minutes of quiet conversation, Mot got up and said clearly to Clare: 'Well, we'll go and get that package for mailing, Clare, and come back and join you in a few minutes. Coming, Gavin?'

'Right,' said Gavin. 'We'll not be long. You can order up a few more juices for us, as we're doing all the work.'

They walked through the shop, saying good-bye to Roddy as they went and telling him they would soon be back with a package for posting which had been forgotten.

Once outside, they strolled casually past the large, black car, with a chauffeur in a peaked hat dozing at the wheel, until they were sure he wasn't watching them. Then they quickly leaped another drystane dyke which bordered the road.

'Did he see us?' said Mot.

'No,' said Gavin. 'He's snoozing!'

'Come on then,' said Mot. 'Let's work our way back until we are near the car.'

He moved slowly and quietly along the dyke, keeping low down and making no sound. Gavin followed him, keeping a good eye out for any old twigs or other objects which might make a noise if he stood on them.

Soon they were level with the car, panting inwardly with the effort of moving silently. They sat down on the grass and tried to peer through chinks in the wall, but could see nothing.

'It doesn't matter,' said Mot. 'It means they can't see us either but we can hear any conversations.'

Gavin looked up at the wall. It was high at that point and they couldn't see the car but they knew by judging the distance before they crossed the wall that they must be beside it.

'Will I look over and be sure it's there?' said Gavin.

'It's taking a risk,' said Mot. 'But we've got to be sure. One look only, then. You're taller than I am so you do it. But slowly and quietly, mind.'

Gavin slowly stood up, but still half-crouching against the stones, looked for a little chink or edge, put his foot in it, reached up for two prominent, sticking out stones and was able to peer over the wall. The car was there almost within touching distance, and the chauffeur still appeared to be sleeping.

He quietly slid down again, and whispered to Mot: 'That's fine. Couldn't be better. We're right beside him.'

'Okay,' said Mot. 'Make yourself comfortable and no movement from now on.'

They settled down on two flat stones and waited with baited breath.

A short time later they heard voices in conversation. One seemed to be one of the men. The other sounded foreign, and must belong to the Ogre.

They seemed to stop at the car because the Ogre said: 'Wake up, Johnstone. I want to be on my way soon. I've just got some business details to settle with our friends here.'

Then there was a silence for a few seconds. Then the voices began again, so close this time that they almost made Gavin and Mot jump. They realised the men were standing very close to the wall, or possibly leaning against it, and that they perhaps didn't want the chauffeur to hear what they were saying.

'It can't be done, just like that,' said the Scots voice.

'They're wild beasts and we shoot at them to kill and are prepared to let wounded deer get away. A stalker can pick out a particular stag but we can't. We haven't time! It's just a question of getting there, shooting, loading the corpses and getting out again.'

The Ogre said: 'Well, I was told on the quiet — and I can tell you I paid plenty for the information — that you knew what you were about and could get deer for anyone, provided there was time and the money was right.'

'That's true,' said the Scots voice. 'But that was meant for the pot, venison for hotels or private customers, not capturing a stag alive.'

Gavin and Mot gulped simultaneously as they realised what had been said.

'Yes,' said the Ogre, 'I appreciate that. But if I were to pay, could you get near to it and knock it out with a tranquilliser dart? You could practically ask your own price.'

There was a silence for a few seconds.

Then the Scots voice said: 'We might be lucky. But it will take some time. But you've got to realise that it will be a stroke of luck. Even experienced stalkers don't always get the stag they are after and they are shooting in the daytime and taking their time to do it.'

'I realise it will be very difficult,' said the Ogre. 'All I'm saying is that as you are going to poach some more deer and if you see this white stag that you don't kill it, but knock it out. I'll pay for all equipment and all expenses. Look, I think we need to talk about this further. Will your men keep quiet? Are they to be trusted?'

'Oh, they're all right. You needn't worry about that aspect. It's just that they don't think you know what is involved.'

The Ogre replied: 'Oh, I know all right. I want that white stag and I'm willing to pay for it alive. I don't want it dead. But I want it!

'Well, I'll have to get going. At least we've established that you are interested. But you'll want to talk money. Why don't you come over tonight, bring one trusted friend with you and we'll settle the details.'

'All right,' said the Scot. 'There's no harm in that. We're still interested and, who knows, we may be lucky. But we'll have to be *very* lucky.'

'I don't believe in luck,' said the other. 'Only in getting what I pay for. Come over about eight o'clock. You know where I am?'

'Yes,' said the Scot. 'It's a deal so far.' He paused for a moment and added: 'I've been asked to do a few deer deals in my time, but this is a new one.'

'Maybe there's not a white stag at all. Maybe it's a ghost,' said the other, adding a grim chuckle.

The Ogre said, with some heat in his voice: 'But

you've seen it! You told me so yourself.'

'Oh, I've seen it,' said the other. 'I was only joking. We all saw it. We fired at it, but missed. It even jumped the bonnet of the car.'

The voices faded as the men moved away from the wall. Then came the noise of a car door closing, an engine starting and the car moved away.

Gavin and Mot let out sighs of relief.

'Whew!' Mot said. 'What a strain! So they are after the white stag! We've got to tell Clare.'

'Yes,' said Gavin. 'We can't let that happen. but where will they go and what will they do? We've no information. We don't know their base or that other chap's. What are we to do? And we didn't take the number of the car.'

Mot pondered. 'Well, we can chew it over for a start and see what Clare can come up with.'

Gavin stretched his legs. It had been a long sit and a strain.

Then he suddenly stiffened.

He leaned forwards and touched Mot's arm and, wordlessly, pointed upwards.

There, above the wall and looking down on them, was a man's face.

CHAPTER 5

Pursued

Gavin couldn't quite decide later on what made him act as he did.

'Creag an Sgairbh!' he suddenly roared and in an instant snatched up a handful of dust and pebbles and hurled them into the red face.

There was a shout of rage and the face disappeared. Gavin leapt to his feet.

'Creag an Sgairbh!' he shouted again, and then raced off along the field in the direction of Roddy's shop, followed by the panting Mot.

As they looked back they saw the man jump the wall and run towards them, but he seemed to find the turf, thistles and stones harder than they did and they gained ground.

'Quick, Gavin, back over the wall!' gasped Mot. 'He'll take longer than us.'

They stopped for a second, then quickly scaled the wall, using nicks and crannies for their feet and hands and dropped down on to the road.

'The shop! The shop! We've got to get to the shop and warn the others,' said Gavin. 'That chap will remember me and he'll know we heard his conversation. We've all got to scarper! He doesn't know our names.'

They sped up the road, and Mot said: 'You're right! You're right! But we haven't got much time to spare. Here he comes again!'

They looked back over their shoulders and saw the man jump heavily down on to the road and begin to run towards them once more.

They ran on round a bend and there was Roddy's shop at the little crossroads at the start of the village and there, too, were cars similar to those Gavin had seen in the lay-by.

As they neared the shop entrance Mot let out the angry 'cackle' a blackbird sometimes gives and repeated it again and again.

Gavin hadn't the breath to try and make any of his bird calls but he burst in through the shop door, past the astounded Roddy and into the tea-room.

The men's heads swung round at the crash of the door and the noise of the running body. Clare and Michael were transfixed.

'Creag an Sgairbh!' bellowed Gavin knowing there was no time for any message. He turned on his heels and bolted out again.

Clare wasted no time on foolish questions. She was quick on the uptake.

She and Michael jumped up and ran to the shop entrance and as she reached the door she, too, shouted the old Clan slogan. She got a glimpse of Roddy's bemused face as the door swung behind her, but there was no time for explanations.

Gavin and Mot were outside the door but ready to speed off in the manner of athletes about to start a footrace. Michael was beside them looking down the road in amazement while a large man with an angry red face pounded towards them with menace written all over him.

'Scatter!' said Clare. 'Go to the den, each his own way!'

The four bodies shot off in different directions; Clare over the wall and across the field towards a birch-wood, Michael straight up the road and into the village, Mot round the side of the shop and across rough ground to where boulders and gorse bushes gave plenty of cover and with the high hillsides beyond. Three separate shouts of 'Creag an Sgairbh!' rent the air.

Gavin was caught napping for a second or two as he tried to make up his mind where to go.

The door of Roddy's shop clanged open as Roddy came out to see what on earth was going on.

The angry man saw Gavin and tried to put on a bit of speed, and his companions tumbled out of the shop, angrily shouting to him to ask what the noise was all about.

Gavin took to the nearest wall like a deer. A running jump, one toe on a projecting stone propelled him upwards, his hands grasped the top, and he was over and thudding down on the grass and heather on the other side.

He was panting hard, but he tried to collect his thoughts.

He was so elated at escaping that he let rip one last 'Creag an Sgairbh!' Long before the man's head came over the wall again he was hidden behind a large stone, lying motionless in a little hollow fringed by heather.

*   *   *   *

Gavin lay motionless, as he had been taught, but with the heather being so thick he thought he would be all right looking through the fronds provided he didn't move around, but he was taking a chance because his face was still white.

He saw one head come above the wall and then three more as the men scanned the ground. He didn't lower his head, merely dropped his forehead forward a little so that his face would not be seen, and stayed still.

He couldn't hear what they were saying but he imagined they were discussing whether to cross over and look for him.

After a few minutes the heads disappeared.

Slowly, very slowly, Gavin lowered his head and sat back in the little hollow. Patience was needed, he knew. He decided to wait there for at least half an hour but it was now late afternoon and he still had to get to the island and then they all had to return to the farm by evening, otherwise there would be a fuss from the adults.

Cautiously, he looked through the heather-fronds again but no one was coming across the moor towards him. His back began to feel damp with the perspiration on his body cooling as he rested and insects began to give him an occasional tiny but irritating bite.

Aunt Elspeth had warned him about these. They were called gnats in England and midges in Scotland and on humid evenings great clouds of them gathered and their bites could drive every person indoors. She had given Gavin a small bottle of anti-midge liquid and he smeared his hands and arms with that, and then his face, taking care to avoid his eyes as the instructions said, and after a time the smarting bites stopped and the midges left him alone.

A small breeze sprang up and that moved them on as it always does, a boon to walkers and fishermen.

He began to study his surroundings, a heather-covered stretch of moorland, with swelling bumps every now and again of boulders which looked as if they had been there for millions of years. When he lay back he could see the back of Ben Ledi and the dark-green of fir plantations, and elsewhere the lighter green of the lovely birchwoods.

Occasionally, a small, brown bird passed over him in a dipping flight, and he made a mental note of these because he knew it was very difficult to distinguish between meadow pipits and tree pipits and even skylarks when one didn't have time to look properly or to use binoculars.

But he enjoyed lying there quietly, watching them pass over, and he was enchanted when a black-and-white bird with a longish tail perched on a boulder and looked down at him, bobbing up and down. He knew that it was a bird of the burns and the moors, a pied wagtail.

Every now and again he carefully looked across the moor to the wall, but he knew the men had gone. The wind made soft sounds in the heather and he put his anorak below his back as the ground was still slightly damp after rain. He began to notice scents and smells and the way lichen on the boulders shone when it was wet, and one particular scent caught his attention and, like the 'feel' of the woods, he was never to forget it. Later Clare told him it was a plant called bog myrtle, which smelled particularly attractive after rain, and it was the plant badge of Clan Campbell.

He lay there in a kind of reverie until he felt he could

move. He looked around with great care, and over towards some woods he saw a large brown bird drifting backwards and forwards and in circles above the trees. He was certain it was a buzzard, and he felt it was safe to move because if anyone had been hiding there, the bird would have gone.

He put on his anorak again and began to think out his next move. If he worked his way along the hillside until he was over a rise, he could see ahead of him. After a bit he could cross over the road and go down through the birchwood to the lochan.

Off he set, moving as quietly as he could. He began to get a little perturbed because light was slightly fading and he had to get to the island and back, and then to the farm before dark.

He picked up a tiny track made by either sheep or deer and began to trot along it until he reached the rise. There he slowed to a walk. He picked his way up through boulders and birch trees until he reached the crest and he could see the line of road far ahead across some more moorland.

The hillsides to his left were much steeper here, broken up into cliffs and rocky sections, and ahead of him was a little knoll.

He saw some movement up ahead and froze. To his intense excitement a large stag with a wide spread of antlers stepped carefully on to the knoll and seemed to survey the ground ahead.

The wind blew from the stag to Gavin and even in his excitement he remembered that if it had been the other way around the stag would have been off. Then, two or three other deer wandered to the top of the mound, grazing as they went.

Then came another, the largest of all, with immense antlers and a lordly air.

Thunderstruck, Gavin saw that it was white.

The white stag slowly turned its head to look towards Gavin, its antlers high and erect.

The other deer had stopped grazing so he must have made some slight sound. The white stag wheeled round and in a few bounds they were up the hillside and over another rise and out of sight.

Gavin gasped. They seemed to flow up the hillside and he realised just how quickly and precisely deer could move over rough ground.

He was getting perturbed by the way time was passing so he half-walked, half-ran, over the moor and across the road and through the wood. He remembered to be cautious and just before going down to the water he scanned the lochan and island. There seemed to be no one around.

He let rip his bird call and it carried over the quiet waters, but the castle and the trees remained silent.

'I wonder if they've gone over?' he said to himself. He tip-toed to the little bay where the galley was kept and there it was, still hidden.

He went back to the birlinn and then he noticed a sign in small twigs and bark placed in the middle of the seat. It was a circle with a dot in the middle and Gavin didn't know what it meant. But Clare and the others were clearly not on the island so Gavin did the sensible thing: he made his way back to the farm and got an amiable but firm ticking-off from Aunt Elspeth for being so late.

Dinner that night was a lively affair. The Clan poured out their adventures to Uncle Fergus.

'Well, you've had a busy day all right,' he said. 'I don't want this stag caught or killed any more than you do, and I detest deer poachers, but all we've got are some general descriptions, bits of conversation. We don't have the car numbers.

'But when I'm in Callander I'll discuss it with the police. In the meantime all of you keep your eyes open.'

There was a chorus of agreement and the conversation turned to other things.

Later, the Clan went up to Clare's bedroom and continued the discussion.

'I was pretty sure you had come back here,' said Gavin. 'But I wasn't entirely sure. What was the meaning of the sign you left on the birlinn?'

'Yes, I'm sorry about that,' said Clare. 'I forgot you wouldn't know all our signs, but it was bright of you to realise that we had come back to the farm. A circle with a dot in the middle means "I-have-gone-home".

'We've got a whole lot like that. I'll give you a list later on, if you like, and you can put them in that old notebook of yours.'

Gavin grinned. He didn't mind his leg being pulled about his notebook: it was packed with useful and interesting material.

'What happened when we all split up?' he asked, still tingling with the thought of that instant flight.

'Oh, they didn't know where to turn first,' said Michael. 'By the time they had made up their minds we had all vanished.'

'Yes,' agreed Mot. 'But they seemed to concentrate on you Gavin. That chap must have remembered you from the lay-by. Or maybe he was still very angry at you throwing dust in his face!'

They all chuckled.

Gavin said: 'I lay hidden for quite a time, I can tell you. But they didn't actually come over the wall. There were so many places I could have gone, and there were so many boulders and so much broken-up ground that they had no idea where to start looking. But I was a bit afraid to start with.'

There was a companionable silence and then Clare said: 'It was lovely that you saw the stag again, Gavin. That really does prove that it is still in this area.'

Gavin nodded. 'Yes, it shook me. The light was beginning to go a bit and perhaps that made it look very white, but I hadn't any doubts that it was the white stag.

'They didn't half go up the hill at speed though, once they saw me.'

Then Gavin remembered something from earlier in the day.

'Clare, what will we do about Roddy? He's bound to be very annoyed at the row we created in his tea-room. We'd better not go down there for a time.'

Clare laughed.

'Oh, Roddy's all right. I went down there earlier this evening and apologised. I said I thought that one of them had objected to you staring at him when they had their cars in the lay-by and I hinted that words had been exchanged, and they were angry because of that. I didn't want to tell him the whole story. He's good fun, but he does talk a lot.

'He said the men had asked him who we were and where we lived. But he didn't tell them. He didn't like the look of them, he said. He told them we were obviously holiday children and that he didn't know where we had stayed in the area but he thought we were going back home as our holiday was over.'

'Good!,' said Mot. 'That will give us a bit of breathing space.'

'Yes,' added Michael. 'It's time we had a proper session getting the hut ready on the island. There's nothing more we can do for a time anyway. It will be sheer chance if we bump into them again.'

'I think we should spend the whole day on the island tomorrow,' said Clare. 'We need a good base and we've got to plan our outing to the top of Ben Buidhe to see the sun coming up and we need a break.'

'Is it a working day tomorrow, Clare?' asked Mot. 'Are we to dress up?'

Clare pondered for a moment.

'Yes,' she said. 'It's time we had a proper Clan ceremony to welcome Gavin and to celebrate our skirmish with these men.

'We'll work, and then we'll have a break and a parade.'

They said goodnight and went to their rooms. Not long before he fell asleep, Gavin looked out of the window at the dark night sky.

He could see the deeper shadow of the hills and pleasant, clean scents came from the moorland outside.

Somewhere, out there, the white stag also slept, its great head tipped forward.

Gavin couldn't explain why, but he suddenly got the feeling, the certain feeling, that they would meet again.

CHAPTER 6

The Meeting of the Clan

Gavin always remembered the next day as a special one. It was the kind of day that sometimes comes, often without warning, to the Highlands in the summer. When he and the Clan left the farmhouse and walked down to the lochan, laden with food and other gear for a full day's stay on the island, the ground underfoot was wet with dew and the hillsides were covered in white mist that slowly drifted and eddied to and fro.

The sky, too, was hidden by a light mist and yet beyond it he could sense the sun was shining and the sky was blue.

Then, bit by bit, the sun grew stronger, the mist and vapour dwindled and died and rolled up the hillsides, which began to show green and grey. By the time they reached the lochan shore it had almost all evaporated and the sun shone brightly.

'It's going to be a scorcher,' said Clare. 'It'll be a great day for doing up the hut.'

Gavin stopped for a second and looked at the hills. He had got into the habit of doing that in the hope he would see more deer, but no matter how often he let his eyes slowly scan the slopes he could make out nothing and he concluded, rightly, that the deer were all high up and lying down in shady hollows sheltering from the heat. But visibility was very sharp, with the bright sun picking out rocks and cliffs and far off hills looking blue and inviting.

It was pleasant getting out on to the cool water and paddling towards the island but it took them two trips with the extra loads.

'Hide the boats well,' said Clare. 'We don't know where these men are and it's just possible they might be snooping around here or even up on the hills.'

'Should we have a fire today?' asked Michael.

'No,' replied Clare. 'It's too hot, and if we want tea we'd better use the stove so there will be no smoke. We can't be too careful at the moment.'

'I agree,' said Mot. 'We'll need to keep a sharp look out at all times from now on.'

Just to be on the safe side Gavin stopped paddling for a second or two and let his eyes scan the hills, but there was nothing but silent hillsides shining in the sun and the green of the still woods.

When they got ashore and had dragged the birlinn and the galley in among the trees, Clare insisted that they be properly camouflaged.

'It's no good ripping up ferns and long grass, Gavin,' she said. 'It soon withers and the different colours catch the eye. It's better to run the boats into the long grass and the trees and then look for broken old branches and cover them with that, but not in a thick heap because that, too, would catch the eye. Just drape a few old branches over to break up the lines and they shouldn't be seen.'

Gavin raked around until he found broken branches and arranged them over the boats until they could not be seen by anyone unless they were especially looking for them.

'Right!' said the masterful Clare. 'To work! We need to finish this roof properly and then think about the inside and some kind of door.'

They went into the room and looked up at the roof.

The cross-pieces seemed quite secure, but the roof needed a proper covering and the inside of the room was slightly damp from rain that had fallen in the night.

Clare went round tugging at the branches and said: 'Well done, Gavin. They are still firm and tight. We now need a good layer of old ferns and branches.'

Seeing Gavin looking puzzled, because it seemed to contradict what she had said about hiding the boats, she added: 'It's all right, Gavin. We need a thick roof to start with and then we can start thinking about how well it fits in to the other ruins.'

She and the others dumped their rucksacks in the little courtyard and, under Clare's direction, they began cutting ferns and long grass until they had a thick heap. Gavin's arms ached as he slashed at the tough roots with his knife and tugged at the grass, but the pile grew and grew until Clare eventually called a halt.

'Break time!' she said. Thankfully, they gathered in the courtyard. Gavin always admired the quiet and efficient way they went about things, with little shouting, arguing, or racket. Mot spread out an old groundsheet. Michael produced little jars or tins of milk and sugar and tea. Clare produced a canister-operated stove and placed it in a sheltered corner and then asked Gavin to take the little kettle down to the lochan and fill it with water.

Obediently, he set off but when he neared the shore he moved cautiously again. He was learning fast. Before going out into the open from the trees and bushes he closely examined the shore opposite and the hillside, but nothing moved.

He waded out a little on a sandy part of the shore and looked down at the clear, cold water. Further out it was brown and peat-coloured, but here it was beautifully clear and he could see little shining pebbles on the bottom. He quickly filled the kettle and headed back for the courtyard.

In a trice Clare had it on the stove, brought it to the boil, tossed in a couple of tea-bags, and soon they were lying around in the sun drinking hot tea which, to Gavin's surprise, both eased his thirst and made him cool.

'If this weather holds, I think we should plan to go up Ben Buidhe tomorrow night,' said Clare. 'I mentioned it to Uncle Fergus and he said to discuss it tonight and perhaps again tomorrow morning when we can see how things will go. It's essential to have a dry night otherwise there's no point in going.'

Gavin thought the idea of sleeping out all night an excellent one.

He asked, 'How will we move in the dark? Isn't it dangerous? We might fall over a cliff or something?'

'No, it's all right,' said Mot. 'It just needs careful planning. It isn't really dark here until very late in the evening and even then there is a kind of light. It will take us about three hours to get up there so we'll leave the farmhouse about seven and get to the top of the hill before ten, that is before dark.'

'And there's a little hollow just down from the top,' said Michael. 'We can get all four of us in there easily.'

'Yes, that's right, said Clare. 'We can all lie down quite easily in our sleeping bags. We try and snatch some sleep and then in the very early morning we get up and watch the sun coming up. Uncle Fergus says it is a marvellous sight.

'We'll leave again in the early hours of the morning and Uncle Fergus will meet us at the roadside just where the track up the mountain comes down to Loch Earn.'

Gavin pondered for a moment. It all sounded fun.

'What will we need?' he asked. 'It must be quite hard going uphill with heavy packs.'

'No, not really,' replied Mot. 'We only need one sleeping bag each, a light groundsheet for putting underneath us, some warm clothing and some food.'

Gavin nodded. He remembered the point about the groundsheet from his last holiday in the Ochils and knew that much overnight damp and cold, even in summer, came up through the ground.

'The sleeping bags will get a bit wet,' said Clare, 'because dew will lie on them overnight, but it doesn't matter for one night and it won't penetrate through. We'll not have to use our compasses because we're not going unless the forecast is certain that the weather and the night will be clear and dry, but we'll have them with us in case we have to navigate back down to the road.'

Gavin let out a small sigh of contentment. 'It sounds fine to me,' he said. 'Who knows, we might see the white stag again.'

By this time the sun was beating down and making the waters of the lochan dance and sparkle, but the chief would allow no more respites.

'All right, back to work,' she said. Mot cleared away the groundsheet and the tins and jars. Michael put the stove on a rock to cool and later put it back in his rucksack and Gavin went into the trees, lifted a large stone, poured the remnants of the tea into the hollow and dropped the stone back. But he gingerly picked up the soggy tea-bags by the corner and took them back to the courtyard and put them on a stone in the sun.

'Good man, Gavin,' said Clare. 'That's the stuff. We'll take them back with us when they're dry and put them in the farm bin.'

Gavin felt a glow of pleasure at the compliment and at remembering the Clan's golden rule: leave no trace of your presence.

Clare supervised the den construction.

'The roof branches are quite secure and they'll hold a thick covering of grass and ferns.

'Mot, you're the lightest. Get up on that wall and we'll hand the stuff up and you can spread it around. Gavin, you get up on that corner there and give him a hand.'

Mot quickly climbed the old wall, finding ledges for his feet and hands and then gingerly moved along the edge of the wall until he found a bit he could sit on. Gavin climbed up as well but only to the first corner.

Clare and Michael began handing up bundles of ferns and grass to Gavin, who spread some on the roof near him and then passed others to Mot who did the same on the other side.

Gradually the roof began to be covered in a thick mat until it looked not unlike the roof of a thatched cottage. Mot took a long stick and raked it around until it was smooth.

'Stay where you are for a moment,' Clare called up. 'I'm going to have a look from the inside.'

Gavin looked around from his perch, glad of the few minutes rest, but he couldn't see much because the ruined walls were still dwarfed by the oak and ash trees and he could only make out bits of hillside through their leaves. But again he did his best to see if anyone was on the shore or the hills.

'You can come down,' said Clare. 'It's looking great. Come and have a look and we'll work out how to make it firm.'

The boys joined her inside the room and looked up. The den was much darker now with the only light coming in through the doorway and the roof was firm and thick with no chinks showing.

'That'll keep out rain all right,' said Clare with satisfaction. 'We'll have to keep some candles in here though, because it will get a bit dark, particularly if we rig up a door. But we've got to weight this roof down in case the wind tears pieces off and to make it less obvious to anyone looking from the shore.'

So the Clan went back to work, lugging long dead branches from all over the island to the castle and Gavin and Mot went back up to their perches. Clare and Michael handed the branches up and they laid them across the grass and ferns, weighting them down and breaking up the pattern of green.

'That's better,' said Clare. 'But we need to finish it off because that green will wither in a day or so.'

Some more raking around produced large pieces of bark which were put on top and then some carefully chosen flat stones were brought from the shore and also placed there.

'Not too many of those,' exclaimed Clare. 'Just enough to weight a corner or two. We don't want them coming through on our heads.'

They sat back and examined their handiwork. It

looked good, thick, natural and well-weighted down, and also firm and secure.

An idea struck Gavin. 'Won't these stones hanging from the ropes swing in the wind and loosen the roof?' he asked.

Clare thought for a moment. 'You're right,' she said. 'We'd better lower them until they are almost touching the ground and then pin them with other rocks. But give them some room to move because wet will make the rope go too tight, like the guy-ropes of a tent.'

Mot and Michael began to cut new lengths of rope and to untie the stones, attach the new sections and then tie up the stones again, and eventually it was done.

Gavin went round placing large stones on the ground on either side of the dangling ones, being careful to give them a little room to move, but blocking them from swinging too much if there was a wind. Again Clare called a halt.

'That's terrific,' she said. 'What a den. Now all we need is a door.

'We'll see if we can get one from the farm and rig it up. We could do with some log seats as well.'

So, perspiring in the sun, the three boys combed the island until they found a couple of suitable logs and, carrying them together, they took them back into the chamber and laid them along the foot of the walls.

Their tins and some rolled-up groundsheets they had brought with them were re-placed inside and the den began to look more like a comfortable base.

'There's easily room for all of us to sleep in here if we wanted to,' said Clare. 'And for our gear as well.'

Satisfied, they returned to the courtyard for lunch. Clare produced a dixie and a packet of dried soup,

Gavin went for water again, and soon they had a bowl of soup each, followed by ginger biscuits and cheese, and then apples and chocolates and more tea.

They lay for ages in the sun, drowsy and reluctant to do any more work. Gavin lay back looking at the blue sky through the green leaves of the trees, shining and infinite, until it began to hurt his eyes.

The afternoon passed in a golden haze, until Clare said: 'We'd better have the parade because we said we would be back by early evening.'

'Must we, Clare?' said Michael. 'It's very hot.'

'Well, it will cool off soon', said Clare. 'It will only take a few minutes. And we did want to have a proper welcome ceremony for Gavin and we really should take a solemn promise on the Holy Iron to defeat these poachers and save the white stag. You never know, we might get the chance.'

Gavin remembered the Holy Iron from his last visit, the promise the Clansmen of past centuries swore on the blade of their long knives called dirks.

He rather liked Clare's desire to have a parade: tartan and knives and solemn promises seemed entirely proper in such a setting and after the events of the past few days.

The boys went through to the den and opened a large tin box and soon they were attired in balmorals with the clan badges on them, to which they each added a sprig of oak leaves and Stewart tartan sashes. Gavin did the same, but he still didn't know what the MacRae plant badge was so he left that alone.

Clare unrolled a groundsheet. Inside were three staves, each brightly painted. She handed Michael and Mot theirs and Gavin eagerly examined them, each with its insignia of birds and animals painted on them, and the top carved into the shape of a bird's head. He desperately wanted one like that.

Clare unwrapped another piece of groundsheet and inside was a tartan cloth. She drew out a long dirk, with a brown Cairngorm stone at one end, and the sheath covered in ornamental designs in something which looked very much like silver.

She called the parade to order. Mot and Michael each stood to attention in the little courtyard and Gavin, after a moment's hesitation, joined them. Clare stood in front holding the jewelled dirk.

'I hereby call this meeting and parade of the Clan Alliance to order. Does that meet with your approval?' she said.

'Aye, it does,' said Mot and Michael. 'Aye it does,' said Gavin a second or two later.

'The Clan Stewart of Appin welcomes our comrade from the Clan MacRae and the Alliance is complete once more. Do you agree?'

'Aye, we do,' said Mot and Michael, with Gavin still trailing behind.

'The task ahead of this Clan is to save the white stag,' said Clare, 'and to stop these poachers. Let us swear to do our best to achieve this.'

She held the jewelled dirk to her lips. 'I so swear,' she said and kissed the blade.

She held it out to Michael and Mot in turn who also said, 'I so swear,' and kissed the blade. Gavin, slightly embarrassed, did the same.

Clare laid the dirk on the ground at her feet and stood to attention with her staff held rather like a spear.

Michael and Mot also came to attention.

'So be it,' said Clare formally. 'For the glory and honour of the Clan.'

Michael and Mot chorused: 'So be it! For the glory and honour of the Clan.'

Clare went into the den, rummaged in the ground-sheet once more and came out with an unpainted and unenscribed staff which she gave to Gavin. 'Uncle Fergus gave me this for you,' she said. 'We'll help you to paint it one night.'

'Gosh, thanks Clare!' said Gavin.

He took the staff and stood to attention like the others.

'Well, that's it,' said Clare. 'Parade dismiss.'

She called out: 'Craig an Sgairbh!'

For the first time that day the Clan's voices reached the shore and the echoes ran gently up the hillsides.

To their consternation, from high up the hill, came the loud report of a rifle shot.

CHAPTER 7

The Ogre Prepares

Clare was the first to react.

'Quick!' she said. 'Get down!'

In a second the Clan Alliance were down behind the castle walls peering anxiously up at the hillsides.

'Take your balmorals off,' hissed Clare. 'We don't want anything glistening or shining. But do it *slowly!*'

Gavin carefully slipped off his balmoral and sash and put them behind a stone and then wriggled over to where Clare, Michael and Mot were huddled behind one of the walls.

Clare was totally in charge.

'You three keep down!' she said. 'I'll keep watch through this crack. There's no need to have four heads bobbing around.'

'All right,' said Michael. 'But tell us what's happening.'

'Otherwise we'll burst,' said Mot.

He, Michael and Gavin sat beside Clare with their backs to the wall and looked up at her as she, half-crouched, peered through the slit.

'There's a man on the skyline,' whispered Clare.

'Take care, Clare,' said Michael. 'Don't let him see you.'

'Don't be an idiot,' said Clare. 'I'm staying behind this crack and there's no light behind me but another wall and he can't make out a thing. He might spot a jerky movement but I'm keeping very still. You three must stay down!'

'All right, Clare,' said Mot. 'You're the boss.'

'The *chief,* please,' retorted Clare.

'Wait a bit! He's off again!'

Michael, Mot and Gavin sat uneasily as tension built up. There was a long silence. Then Clare said: 'He seems to be looking for someone or something. He's moving backwards and forwards across the hillside. He's got a stick or staff as well, I think. I wish I could see better.'

'Do you want my binoculars?' asked Gavin.

'Good idea,' said Clare. 'But just a second! I don't want the sun glinting on anything and giving us away.'

She glanced round.

'It should be all right. The sun is on him and not on me. Crawl over and get them out of your rucksack, Gavin, but wrap them up in something so there's no shine.'

Obediently, Gavin crawled across the courtyard, keeping close to the wall, until he got to his rucksack. He made sure he was totally hidden from the hillside and took out his binoculars, wrapping them in his jersey.

He crawled back to Clare and handed them over, and squatted down again behind the wall.

Clare very slowly adjusted the focus and looked carefully through the slit.

She gave a sudden gasp.

'It's not a stick!' she said. 'It's a rifle! He's casting around looking for something but I can't see what. The hillside is very broken up there with lots of little rocky bits among the heather.'

There was another taut silence.

Then she gasped again. 'He's coming down lower. He's looking this way.'

Another silence.

Then she whispered: 'It's all right, he was just looking around. He hasn't seen us. What on earth is he up to? If he's shooting at deer he's up to no good. And if he's one of the poachers we've got to do something.'

Michael tugged at Clare's arm.

'Is he one of the men we saw? Can you make out any features, Clare?'

'He's a bit far out yet,' Clare said. 'But I didn't really get a good look at him before. Only Gavin has seen them twice.'

'Let me have a look, Clare' whispered Gavin.

'All right,' said Clare. 'But slowly, mind, and carefully.'

She handed the binoculars to Gavin and sat down at the foot of the wall, making room for him to crouch behind the narrow crack in the stonework.

He focused the binoculars and the green hillside through the crack sprang sharply into view. He picked out the man and could see he was standing still on top of a large boulder, the rifle held slant-wise across his chest, and seemed to be examining the hillside below him.

Gavin couldn't see his face clearly, but the build of the man looked familiar.

'Clare!' he said without moving his head and still keeping the man in full view. 'It's very like the man we saw over the wall, the one who chased us after I flung the dust at him.'

He continued to look, but began to blink a little with

the difficulty of trying to use binoculars through a small gap while at the same time remaining motionless.

Then the man looked up and Gavin, who had become quite good now at noticing detail, was sure it was the same one.

For the second time in a few days he found himself telling Clare that he could identify one of the men.

'Yes, it's him,' he whispered. 'It's the same one who chased us. Or if it isn't, then he's got a double.'

'What's he doing now?' asked Mot.

Gavin was silent for a minute and then said: 'He's coming down the hill, but slowly.'

Then it was his turn to gasp.

'Wait a bit! There's something down below him. There's a lot of trees there, birches I think, and there's something moving in that.'

The tension grew, then Gavin exclaimed: 'It's a deer! But he hasn't seen it. He's looking along the hillside in a different direction.'

Then, before he could stop himself, he yelped. 'Gosh!'

Clare, Michael and Mot all hissed in unison for him to be quiet.

'Sorry!' whispered Gavin. 'But it's the stag! The white stag! It's moving very slowly. Here, Clare, you have a look.'

Clare, quietly took the binoculars from him. She gazed silently for a moment and then said: 'You're right! It's well in among these birches so I can't get a proper look. But there's a clear bit further down and it seems to be heading for that. The man above can't see it because it is just below a little cliff and the slope is cutting off his view.'

She re-scanned the hillside. Then it was her turn to gasp. 'There's another three of them coming down the hillside,' she said. 'They're just above the first man.

'Now they're together. They seem to be discussing something.' She paused, then added, 'The first man is pointing along the hillside.' She paused again.

'Well, tell us! Tell us!' said Mot. 'What's happening? What are they doing?'

'They're spreading out in a line and coming down the hill,' said Clare.

She fiddled with the focus on the binoculars for a second and then said: 'Got it! It's clear of the trees and on an open bit. It's the white stag, all right! It's stopping and turning round. Why isn't it running away fast? These men will catch up with it soon.'

'Should we shout and yell and let them know they have been seen?' asked Michael. 'It might scare them off.'

'Yes, we've got to do something,' added Mot.

'Hang on,' said Clare. 'They're a bit up the hill yet.'

Her eyes, too, began to water and she whispered for Gavin to come back to the crack and she handed him the binoculars.

'It's the small space,' she said. 'It makes it difficult to see sometimes and if the focus catches the edges of the crack that seems to affect your eyes.'

Gavin took her place and quickly found the line of men.

'They've halted,' he said. 'Now they're off again. They're still coming down but very slowly. They're all spread out in a line.'

He moved the binoculars slightly and found the stag, this time crossing an open space, large and white in the sun and with its huge spread of antlers nodding slightly as it moved forward.

Then it swung round and descended a little gully and Gavin let out another exclamation.

'What is it?' quietly asked Clare.

'It's been shot,' gasped Gavin. 'It's got a long red streak across one shoulder and it's limping slightly.'

'The villains!' muttered Clare. 'They'll pay for this.'

Michael and Mot looked anxiously at Gavin.

'Where is it now?' asked Mot.

'It's reached a flat bit,' said Gavin. 'Ah, that's better. It's started to gallop, but slowly. It must have found descending the steep bits very painful. 'The men still can't see it. Drat it, my eyes are watering again.'

He and Clare slickly changed places, and Clare kept up the commentary.

'Yes, it's speeding up a bit. There's a long flat bit of moorland on the left there, just to the side of the hill and that line of birches coming down the hillside will hide it.

'It's going to get away. Yes. I've lost it. It's over a couple of hummocks and well out of sight. They won't get it now.'

The boys could not resist a small cheer.

'Quiet, you idiots,' said Clare. 'We don't want them to hear us. We want to see what they are going to do next so we can report them.

'They're very near the shore now. Take the binoculars, Gavin, and keep out of sight. I don't need the binoculars any more. Not a sound from anyone!'

She continued to look through the small gap but only after she had scraped up some dirt from the courtyard floor and rubbed her face with it. She remained totally still, and Gavin recalled two points about the outdoors, how white a face can look, even at a distance, and how important it was to stay motionless.

The men gathered on the shore and one of them pointed to the island.

They seemed to be discussing it and the sound of their voices carried over the water but the Clan could not make out what they were saying.

Then they turned and moved off along the shore and were soon lost in the trees.

'Whew!' said Clare. 'That was close!'

* * * *

Later that evening a group of men gathered in the drawing room of a mansion house about ten miles away from Faskally. The curtains were drawn and the lights were shaded.

Sitting in an armchair was the Ogre, and facing him were three of the men.

'Well?' demanded the Ogre. 'What happened?'

The men shifted uneasily, glancing at one another. 'You tell me, Buchanan,' said the Ogre. 'You're the leader.'

'My name is Buck for short,' the man briskly replied and then seeing the Ogre was clearly in no mood for idle chatter he hurriedly continued.

'We were poaching and there were so many police patrols on the road we had to send our vehicles off with only the drivers and we hid up on the hillside for the rest of the night.

'We arranged to be picked up the next morning in that little lay-by where we once had a puncture not far from that little loch with the old castle.'

'Okay, okay,' said the Ogre. 'Cut that detail. Tell me what happened later.'

Buck leaned forward: 'You are paying us well for this job,' he said. 'But you've got to listen to what I have to say. We know these hills. You don't! We've got to be careful as well. There was a bunch of nosy holiday kids listening in to our conversation the other day and I'm told they've all gone home now but we can't be too careful.'

The Ogre relaxed a little. 'Yes, I know,' he said. 'You're the best at getting deer and not getting caught, and I know I've given you a hard task. But I'm paying you well.'

'There's no complaint about that,' said Buck. 'But here's what happened.

'We were descending the hill and trying to look like hill-walkers, with the rifle wrapped up to look like a staff, when we came over a mound and there, right in front of us, was the white stag.'

'What!' said the Ogre, jerking upright.

'Yes,' said Buck. 'But is was all so sudden. It was stuck in a peat-bog and had been thrashing around and it was partly covered in mud. It wasn't clear to us right away that it was the white stag.

'Anyway, Willie whipped the cover off the gun just as it clambered clear and took a shot at it.'

The Ogre glared in anger, and Buck hurriedly continued: 'I knocked his arm up and the bullet only scored its shoulder. But it is wounded and I reckon it will recover but for a day or two it will lie up somewhere. I reckon we could get it now with a tranquilliser. But you've got to be ready with your Land-Rover, tarpaulins, horse-box on the road and all the rest.'

The Ogre nodded slowly, a pleased gleam in his eyes.

'No problem! I'll lay all that on here, ready to move when you give the word. What do you think the chances of getting it are?'

'Slightly better than 50-50,' Buck said. 'We lost it today but it won't go far with that shoulder.

'But there's more! Willie's shot knocked it over and I managed to hit it with a tranquilliser dart. It was so close to us and it was all so sudden. The dart fell out again so the drug will only partly have affected it. But it will slow it down.

'We'll go back there at first light tomorrow. I reckon it's in that flat bit of moorland, just down from the hill and along a bit from the lochan. There's a lot of hollows in there, just the place for it to hole up.'

The Ogre grunted in pleasure.

'Well, that's a turn up for the book. All right, when you find it, hide it safely and ring me here. Then we can make arrangements to get it to the vehicle. But I want it alive and unharmed. If it dies, there's no bonus.'

'Yes, we know,' said Buck. 'That's not an easy part either. If it's lying drugged then hooded crows or ravens could have a go at its eyes, or foxes or buzzards will think it is dead or dying and attack it.

'But we've got some time to spare. When we find it I'll have a man beside it always.'

Buck stopped for a moment and then said: 'You must be very keen on getting it alive. Is it for a private zoo? It's bound to be something like that.'

The Ogre glared again: 'I don't want questions like that. What I intend to do with it is my affair.

'But I'll tell you this much. I'm only acting for a millionaire who has one of the best private zoos in the world and within 24-hours of the white stag being taken alive it will be flown out of the country to France.

'It will be looked after there for some time and then flown to the States. And I'm only telling you that much so you know that money isn't a problem.'

'All right,' said Buck. 'I only asked. But we'll handle our end of the deal. Now we'd better get on our way.

'We want to be back on the hillside the minute it gets light. But we'll stick to only using four men though, just enough to put it in the tarpaulins we've prepared.

'I've had a kind of hammock made as well, which four, or perhaps six, men could put the stag in and then carry it.

'If we have to, I could use one of those small hill tractors but they're noisy and will attract attention. But that's only for emergencies.'

'Excellent,' said the Ogre. 'You'd better get on your way.

'But just one last point. If you do get it today, where will you hide it until I can get the vehicles to you?'

Buck replied: 'I've got all that worked out. There's an old bothy — an empty cottage — in a glen nearby. No one goes there except in the stalking season and that's some time away and the door can be locked.'

He paused.

Then he added: 'And there's that ruined old castle on the lochan. We could hide it there as well, if we had to.

'We've been keeping an eye on that.'

CHAPTER 8

Night on the Hill

There was a great to-do in Uncle Fergus' house that night. Gavin and the others poured out their story about the men, the stag and the shot they had heard.

Uncle Fergus listened intently and then went and phoned the police.

He came back and told the children: 'Well, they'll do what they can. They're increasing their night patrols on the roads but they are getting reports of poachers in other areas so they are a bit stretched.

'They are going to make inquiries about a foreign visitor hiring or renting a house here and they will question him.

'The trouble is that he may not even be staying in this area but has driven here from some other place. Each year many foreign guests rent houses here, or he may be staying with friends or staying in hotels.

'It's not much to go on, but they'll do what they can. In the meantime, you lot keep your eyes open. You've done very well so far. But don't tangle with them. Keep clear of trouble and tell me immediately you see them again or anything else odd.'

The Clan Alliance promised faithfully to do that and the talk turned to other things.

Uncle Fergus told them he had sent the piece of

brass chain Clare had found on the island to a museum in Edinburgh.

'It's almost certainly part of a sporran chain,' he said. 'It might be 17th century and they want a good look at it so they'll keep it for some time. The little sharp spearhead was used for spearing salmon and it's not very old at all so you can have that back if you like and if you are careful with it.'

He handed it to a grateful Michael who said he would make a new shaft for it, and immediately enlisted Gavin's help to try it out on the loch trout at the first available opportunity.

Then the Clan took themselves off upstairs and continued planning and plotting as they worked at various tasks.

Clare was busy painting a piece of bone black. 'What on earth is that, Clare?' asked Gavin.

'It's a woggle,' said Clare. 'You know the kind of thing Scouts and Cubs use round their neck scarf, but this is an old bone from the neck of a sheep.

'You can find them around if you look for them. I brought it home in a bag as it was a bit smelly. Look, it's got a hole right through it.'

Gavin examined it and saw it was very roughly in the shape of a butterfly and had a hole in the middle.

'What are you going to do with it?' he asked.

'I thought it might make a nice attachment to the end of our sashes,' said Clare. 'They're always flapping about at the ends once we tie them on, but if we pass the ends through the hole here, like a neck woggle, it will keep them tidy. And I thought I would glue on a tiny clan-badge. Look!'

She showed Gavin one of the attractive belt-and-buckle clan brooches he had seen in Scottish shops, just like the big one he had for his balmoral, but this one was tiny and had the Stewart of Appin emblem.

He thought the idea was an excellent one and made up his mind he would get one too.

'We'll come across sheep corpses as we walk around,' said Clare. 'They smell terribly, so you've got to poke out this bone with a stick and leave it for some days.

'Then, when you bring it back, you've got to scrub it in boiling water and disinfectant until it is perfectly clean. Then it can be painted.'

She worked away until it was all coated in shiny black paint and then put it on a shelf to dry.

Gavin began to work at his staff. He decided he would leave the head rounded and try and carve the face of an owl on one side. There were four knot-holes in the staff, where branches or twigs had once been and he worked at these with a knife and some old sandpaper until he had made them into little flat circles.

'That's not bad, Gavin,' said Mot. 'But take it easy. It's a mistake to do too much in one night.'

'Yes, that's right,' said Michael. 'You then hurry on and make mistakes. It's better to do a little section each evening you have some spare time.'

'All right,' said Gavin. 'I just thought I would do the knot-holes first, and then the head and then cut some circles and whorls in the bark further down.'

'Fine!' said Mot. 'But don't draw anything on the knot-holes until you have finished carving the top. Always work from the top down.'

'Yes,' chimed in Clare. 'And always draw your carving or design on paper first, to the same size, so you can see if it will work out or not.'

Gavin said he would follow all this excellent advice, so he spent the rest of the evening drawing the main features of an owl's face, copied from his bird book, on to a piece of paper.

He found that simple things were best, a round line for the face, then the eyes, and beak, and he was surprised to find he could get a good owl's face without too many lines.

'It's just as well,' said Clare. 'It's one thing drawing them and quite another carving them in wood. It's got to be simple. All you need are the main features in outline.'

So Gavin studied his drawing and the top of the staff and with a piece of chalk he marked which bits he would carve out and which he would leave.

Michael came to his rescue. 'Here, catch this,' he said, tossing Gavin a piece of wood similar in size to the top of the staff.

'Draw your owl's head on that, and then have a go at carving it. Watch your fingers, mind. When you've finished that piece of wood here's a couple of others and you can work on them as well.

'Don't touch your staff until you are certain you can make a success of it.'

'Great!' said Gavin who had been secretly worried about making a mess of it all.

'And here's something else, too,' said Clare, handing him some plasticine. 'Try modelling your owl's head, then try carving it on the old pieces of wood. You'll find that a help.'

So Gavin worked away with his plasticine and old wood, muttering to himself as his designs failed or he cut off bits he really wanted to leave on, and he found himself clumsy and inexpert. But he began to learn.

Gradually, as the evening passed, and Clare, Michael and Mot read or chatted, he got very close to producing a shape on an old piece of wood that was reasonably owl-like.

Then Uncle Fergus brought it all to an end by shouting up the stairs: 'Supper's ready! And I want to discuss your Ben Buidhe trip. We can't be too careful at the moment if these men are around.'

So the Clan tumbled down the stairs to eat a huge supper and to hold a Council-of-War.

It did not have a very happy beginning.

Uncle Fergus gathered the Clan round the kitchen table and told them that he and Aunt Elspeth had wanted to cancel their night visit to the top of Ben Buidhe.

'We've been discussing it at some length,' he told the sad-faced group. 'It's a big hill, there's these odd men around and we felt you are still a bit on the young side to go up there on your own at night.'

'But . . . ' said Clare, trying to cut in, but she was hushed by Uncle Fergus.

'Oh, yes, I know, Clare,' he said. 'You feel you can navigate your own way around but there's some very wild country down the back of the hill.

'That's the bad news.'

They looked expectantly at him.

'Now for the good news. We've decided to let you go . . . '

A cheer broke out from the children.

Uncle Fergus went on: 'But only on certain conditions. The forecast says it will be a dry and clear night, it should also be good tomorrow and I will come up to the top of the hill with you.'

The children's faces fell again. A grown-up! It would take the sense of adventure away.

He went on: 'I'll see you settled into that little hollow near the top — you know it, Clare, from previous visits — and then I'll go down again. The path down is quite clear and I'll meet you on the road around eight a.m. If by some chance you are down earlier than that then you can doze by the roadside. But don't be late.

'If you were to stray from the path you know that by using your compasses and going due north you would strike the road and you would know where you were without any doubt.

'But I want an assurance, Clare, that you will not go wandering down the back of the hill. It is really very wild there, with many peat bogs, and rough moorland, and we don't even use the old bothy there now.'

Seeing Gavin looking puzzled, he added, 'A bothy is a small cottage, Gavin, and this one was built many years ago and was used in the deer stalking season. It is still in quite good condition and we keep the door closed to keep the sheep out, but it is not used now since forestry planting made the deer in that area shift their ground. A new bothy was built in another glen.

'But back to the trip. Would that suit you all?'

There was a chorus of agreement.

Aunt Elspeth came in at that point, smiling at the hubbub.

'So far I've left it to you, Uncle,' she said. 'Now it's my turn. Don't get into trouble or I'll never forgive you, nor could I face your parents. But we've got a lot of work to do before you set off this evening, so it's all hands to work.'

She allocated tasks, Clare to see to the sleeping bags and groundsheets, Mot and Michael to make sandwiches, Gavin to look out items like thermos flasks, midge-cream, and warm jerseys and other extra clothing.

It turned out to be an unforgettable night, and many years later Gavin still remembered the line of figures slowly trudging up the path, rucksacks on their backs, Uncle Fergus leading the way. No one spoke, but every now and again one or other of them would point out deer on knolls or on the skyline, or peering down at them from the ridges like Apache scouts in films.

Once they rounded a bend and a large stag and two hinds stood looking at them and then moved slowly up the hillside. Their coats were beautiful rich chestnut brown.

'They are in peak condition,' whispered Uncle Fergus. 'We've a good bit to go yet before we get into the peak of stalking so they are not too wary at the moment.'

All the time they kept a good look-out for the white stag, but no one saw it.

Then they reached the top. It was very late in the evening but they could still see what they were doing. All around were range after range of hills, blue-black in the evening light. Gavin had never seen such wild country and he was fascinated.

They found the little hollow just down from the summit and Uncle Fergus let Clare make the arrangements.

'There's just room for the four of us lying full-length,' she said. 'Put the groundsheets down first, Gavin. I know it is a dry night but cold and damp always come up through the ground in the night. There will be dew as well in the night and early morning and that will make the top of the bags damp but it won't matter for one night.'

They spread the groundsheets as directed and then Uncle Fergus said: 'Well, I'll leave the rest to yourselves. No wandering around the hillsides in the dark, stick to the path in the morning and, on no account, are you to go exploring down the back to the wild area. Well, best of luck!'

They all said they would do as they were told, and watched his tall figure quickly tramp downhill. Soon he was out of sight as the track went round a ridge.

Clare continued to mastermind the operation. She had her rucksack made out of half of a sailor's canvas bag with the top drawn together with cord and a plastic bag inside that, and the frame was made from deer-antlers. Gavin thought it looked great and he determined he would make one too.

She slipped the antler-frame off, took out the plastic bag and placed it beside her.

'It's a good idea to place the bottom of your sleeping bag inside your rucksack, Gavin,' she said. 'That way, you ensure your feet are warm and dry and get a good night's sleep.

'It's also a good plan to rub your feet with a clean towel and slip on a fresh pair of socks, but do that inside your bag in case you accidentally stand on the turf and get those damp, too.'

Gavin noted these points, and they all placed their plastic bags in a little pile, tucking the ends in. They seemed to be old bin-liners, Gavin noted, and the ends could be knotted over what was inside.

They wriggled inside their bags, put on extra jerseys and lay back in comfort.

'This is marvellous,' Gavin thought to himself as he looked up at the night sky, his head comfortably relaxing on an old jersey he was using as a pillow.

As the light began to dim, the stars appeared and Mot and Michael began to point them out to him. The Plough was easy, with its saucepan-like shape, and Gavin was quickly able to follow the line of the two end stars and then pick out the North Star, which is such a help in navigation.

'It's a useful thing to learn,' said Clare. 'Sometimes we try it in the autumn or early winter when the stars are big and bright. When you get to know where the constellations are at different times of the year, and you can see some of them, you can soon pick out north, south and east and west even if cloud is hiding the Plough and the North Star.'

They pointed out the bright stars which make up the heads, arms and feet of Orion, the Hunter, with Sirius, the bright dog star at his heel, and Gavin could easily make out the stars which made up his belt. Another easy one to spot was the 'W' shape of Cassiopeia and so was the Seven Sisters.

They discussed this in lazy tones until Clare said they should sleep. 'I've brought the small alarm clock,' she said. 'Some parties have come up here to see the sun rise and have then slept through it. I've set it for the very early morning.'

Night haze began to drift across the sky and it grew markedly cooler. Gavin noticed that both Michael and Mot had put on light balaclavas as caps and he did the same and snuggled deep down into his sleeping bag.

There were no sounds except the occasional sigh of the night wind and an occasional deep bark from deer deep in the corrie below them.

Gavin drifted off to sleep. When the alarm went he was startled for a few minutes because he didn't know where he was. Instead of bedroom walls and ceiling there was a grey sky. The sleeping bag and the ground were wet with dew and a vapour-like mist covered many of the higher hills. But to the east it looked more clear, but very grey.

The rest of the Clan began to stir. 'We've still plenty of time,' said Clare. 'I suggest we have a proper breakfast.'

They dug out their flasks and sandwiches and gradually came awake as they ate.

As Gavin gazed around, he noticed that the mist on the hills began to drift very slowly upwards and he got that lovely feeling that the day was going to be very dry and sunny.

Michael and Mot took their boots and stockings from inside the plastic bags, put them gingerly on the wet ground and tried to get into them without getting damp. Gavin did the same and soon all four stood up.

'It's still very cold,' said Michael, gazing around. 'It sure is,' agreed Mot. They all donned anoraks or cagoules, and Clare suggested they go to the top of the hill and walk around to keep warm.

This they did, talking quietly in whispers, and enjoying the feeling of being in a really wild place, with the hills all around. Gradually the sky to the east began to lighten.

'Not long now,' said Clare. Michael and Mot were trotting backwards and forwards on the flat top of the hill, slapping their arms across their chest.

'Thank goodness for that,' said Mot. 'I'm freezing!'

Gavin, too, felt it was cold, surprisingly so for the summer and he had at that stage still to learn just how low temperatures can drop high up in the hills, even in summer.

Then they all stopped as if transfixed.

The far horizon to the east grew bright, golden yellow and, as they watched, a line of bright apple-green appeared over the hills, but only for a second or two, and then there was a flash of brilliant red and the sun appeared, golden and shining. Its rays lit up their faces and removed the shadows from the rocks and cliffs and, suddenly, everything was shining and golden. It had only taken a few seconds but Gavin thought it was one of the most beautiful things he had seen.

They leaped up and down and though they did try and be quiet on the hills they could not help a muted cheer.

'Great!' said Clare. 'Marvellous!'

They all made similar expressions of pleasure and returned to their sleeping bags and had some more tea and a sandwich or two. 'Keep one or two as reserves,' called Clare. 'You never know.'

Gavin noticed that the mist-vapour was quickly vanishing from the hills and the dew from the ground.

'It's going to be a scorcher of a day,' he said. 'Yes, it is,' replied Clare. 'We can have a sleep later on but there's still plenty of time for other things. I suggest we go over to the island again: we've still got some work to do there.'

Mot and Michael agreed, and it seemed a good idea to Gavin, too.

'What's the time, Clare?' he asked. 'It's about six,' she said. 'We've plenty of time to get down the track to the road, but we should move off fairly soon.'

After a bit they began to re-pack their rucksacks and were soon ready to move; 'saddled up', Mot put it.

When Gavin was packing his rucksack he noticed he had put his binoculars in on top and he turned to Clare and said: 'I wouldn't mind a last look from the summit, Clare, if that's all right.'

'Sure,' she said. 'Don't wander too far, though.'

Gavin clambered up the slope to the top and stood beside the cairn for a bit and looked around at the hills, glens and moors spread out before him. The top was large and grassy and he walked to the edge and peered down. Twice he saw tiny orange-brown specks far below and when he turned his binoculars on them he could see they were deer.

He wandered over to the south side which looked over the wild country which Uncle Fergus had cautioned them about. The sun suddenly glinted on something in the far distance.

He focused his binoculars on it and saw he was looking at a tiny cottage tucked away in a green fold in a glen with what looked like a rough track leading to it and which then ran away to the south and disappeared from his view.

It looked a very lonely spot and he remembered Uncle Fergus saying that the estate didn't use the bothy any more.

'I can see the old bothy,' he called to the others as they came over the brow of the hill.

'Oh, can you?' said Mot. 'Let's have a look.'

He borrowed the binoculars from Gavin and gazed for a time. 'It still looks in not bad condition,' he said.

Michael also had a look and said: 'What's that place

called again, Clare? I always thought it sounded like a sneeze.'

Clare chuckled, 'It's called A'Chuill and it means the back-bothy, or the bothy down the back. It's pronounced Ach-hool, Gavin.'

Gavin took another look. He blinked and looked again. Then, in front of the startled eyes of Clare, Mot and Michael, he suddenly threw himself down flat.

Quick on the uptake, the others followed, but more slowly, and Gavin mentally kicked himself for forgetting to avoid jerky movement. 'What is it?' said Clare.

'There are men at the bothy,' said Gavin.

'What?' said Michael. 'Are you sure?'

'Of course I'm sure,' said Gavin. 'I can see them.'

He handed the binoculars over again and they all looked in turn.

'You're right,' said Clare. 'How odd! No one is supposed to go there now.'

Gavin continued to look. Then he gasped. 'A Land-Rover or a vehicle like that has just come round the bend,' he said. 'It's stopping at the bothy. They're lifting out something heavy.

'I can't quite make it out because some of them are standing in front of it. There are about four or five men in all, I think.

'Ah, that's better. They seem to be talking. If one of them would move for a second I could get a decent look.'

He gasped again.

'Clare, they've got what looks like an animal on a kind of sheet and they are dragging it into the bothy.' He looked again. 'It's like a stag,' he said quietly.

'Now they're closing the door. They're all getting into the vehicle.'

Another pause. 'They're moving off again but very slowly. Now it's round the bend. I can't see it any more.'

He put the binoculars down and said, very gravely: 'Clare, I can't be absolutely sure. It looked very much like a stag.

'And it was white.'

CHAPTER 9

The Lonely Bothy

Clare took command.

'We've got to do something about this,' she said. 'We've got to find out what's going on.'

'Quick, ideas, please!'

The others looked blank-faced at one another and then Mot said: 'We'll have to go down there and see. It all looks very fishy. It's bound to be them.'

Gavin added: 'It certainly did look like a stag. It's terrible! I hope it isn't dead. Imagine shooting something like that.'

His face darkened with anger.

'It's evil!' he said. 'We've got to stop them. And even if there's a normal explanation it has to be checked out.'

Michael chimed in 'I agree! But what are we to do? That's the very wild area. We promised not to go there.'

Gavin and Mot glanced at one another and then Mot said: 'But it's an emergency! Perhaps if one of us went and the rest stayed here that would be all right?'

Gavin said: 'But we'll use up time and Uncle Fergus will be waiting for us at the road and will get worried if we don't show up. Suppose we get held up for ages — he could get very worried and even start to organise a search. And we did promise.'

There was a moment's silence while they all frantically thought what to do and then Clare exclaimed:

'I've got it! We promised not to go wandering around but we are not going to do that.

'We can see the bothy and we are only going straight there and the day is going to be very hot and clear. In any case, a track runs from the bothy to the Strathyre road and Uncle Fergus knows we will be safe walking along that and if it all works out he can meet us on it.

'The track is quite hard to spot where it links with the road because it is rarely used nowadays and is well screened by trees, Uncle Fergus knows it all right.

'But someone will have to go down and tell him what is happening.'

They all turned and looked at Mot.

'Oh no,' he said. 'Not me! The last time something like this happened, I had to go and get help.

'It's someone else's turn!'

Clare grinned.

'It doesn't happen that often,' she said. 'But you're the quickest mover on the hill and particularly going downhill, so it will have to be you.'

'Oh, all right,' said the reluctant Mot. 'You're the boss. What do you want me do do?'

'You've to wait at the road for Uncle Fergus and tell him what we have seen. You're to tell him we have gone down to A'Chuill bothy, that we can see our way clearly and are not wandering around.

'Tell him we hope to see what is going on and we will then go back to the Strathyre road by the bothy track.

'You'd better tell him to bring some other men with him. If it is the poachers they might be quite a tough lot.'

She paused: 'And tell him we are being very careful and will stay out of sight.'

'Fine!' said Mot. 'Anything else?'

Clare thought for a moment.

'No, I think that's all. Keep your eyes peeled going downhill. There maybe more of them around.'

'All right,' said Mot, hitching on his rucksack. 'I'm off.'

Clare had an afterthought. 'Have you any food left?' she said.

'Yes,' said Mot. 'I've some sandwiches and an apple.'

'Well, spin it out,' said Clare. 'We don't know what kind of day we've got ahead of us or when we'll eat again so don't gobble it up.'

'Right, Clare,' said Mot. 'Best of luck everyone!'

'See you, Mot,' said Gavin, trying to be calm, though inwardly his heart was pounding with excitement.

'Yes, good luck, Mot,' said Michael.

'Are we all ready too?' asked Clare, looking around.

Michael and Gavin were crouched down and their rucksacks were on.

Mot was already on the edge of the summit top, ready to go down. He turned just as Clare, Gavin and Mot moved to the other edge. They turned for a second and looked at one another, still keeping down so as not to be seen on the skyline.

Mot raised his hand in farewell.

'Creag an Sgairbh!' he called quietly.

'Creag an Sgairbh!' they chorused.

'Right!' said Clare, 'let's go to war!'

And she led the way over the brow of the hill.

*   *   *   *

The Clan, minus Mot, crouched behind a heathery knoll and closely eyed the bothy. They had made good speed descending the hill, skilfully making use of the peat hags and little hollows in the ground so that they were not seen from below, until they reached a long cut-out section which had been made by a burn and they were safe from view.

'This will do fine,' said Clare. 'It will take us close to the bothy so we can have a good look. But stay low and no talking and check your rucksacks so that nothing rattles.'

They crept slowly along the bed of the now dried-up burn and Gavin's heart nearly stopped when they rounded a bend and a bird suddenly shot up beside him and soared away cackling 'Go-back, go-back'.

'Drat it!' said Clare. 'Grouse always make such a racket. Sit down for five minutes and stay quiet. If there's anyone at the bothy they will just think it was disturbed by a fox or something natural.'

They sat quietly in a row, listening intently. Gavin could hear nothing but the occasional swish of a slight breeze in the heather and a very faint noise which Clare whispered to him was probably a far-off waterfall.

Clare very slowly raised her head above the level of the bank and hissed: 'It's all quiet. Keep going!'

They wriggled their way along the bed of the burn and Gavin was intrigued to see that at one point a little spring of clear water had sprung up and a small burn began. Then he could see the roof of the bothy above the level of the bank and Clare halted again.

'One of us should go forward and see if there's anyone there. Gavin, you saw them best before and can recognise any of them. Do you think you can do it? Can you wriggle to the back of the bothy and get a look through that window at the side?'

Gavin gulped a little. 'Yes, Clare. I think I can do that. But what happens if we are spotted?'

'We run for it,' said Clare. 'But we've got to run together this time and stay together. If, by some chance, one of us looks like getting caught then the rest can split up in different directions but we've got to come together again. If we are scattered, then work your way back to this burn where we are now. The bothy can always be seen, so there is little danger of anyone getting lost. And they won't expect us to come back here but will be looking around close to the track.

'Off you go!'

Gavin checked that he had nothing about him that would shine or make noises and then wriggled over the bank and began to crawl through the heather towards the back of the bothy. Every now and again he lay quiet until he could get his breath and to stop his heart pounding.

He listened carefully but could hear nothing and then he was right up against the back of the bothy and he crouched there for a second or two while he gathered his thoughts. He could see the edge of the banking that hid Clare and Michael but could not see them, though he knew they were experts at hiding. The stone walls of the bothy were partly sheltered by high sections of moorland so unless someone actually walked right round the bothy he was fairly safe from view.

Gavin worked his way slowly round the side of the bothy and then carefully — very carefully — he slowly raised his head until he could peer in the window. He could see a room, rather dark because the one window only let in a little light, and something large lying on the floor, covered by a tarpaulin.

There seemed to be no one inside.

He wriggled his way round to the front door and still could see no one. Then he crawled to the moorland at the side of the bothy and had a good look round. The men appeared to have gone.

Very gingerly he went to the door and tried the handle. It was locked, but there was a key in the lock. He turned it carefully with a little click and went inside.

His eyes got accustomed to the gloom and he could see at the back there was a kind of partition stretching about halfway to the roof and behind it were old planks, fencing stobs, a broken table, some larger sheets of wood which he thought might have been left there at some time to complete the partition, and other junk. It was all very dusty and dirty and covered at the sides in cobwebs.

But that was only a quick glance. The thing that transfixed him was the large object lying on the floor.

It was covered with a tarpaulin and as his eyes got accustomed to the light he could see what looked like a head and large antlers sticking out of one side and he could hear a steady noise which sounded like breathing.

Apprehensively, he tugged back a corner of the tarpaulin and there was the white stag, eyes closed, great head slumped and its sides heaving with a deep, steady breathing.

Gavin shot out of the door like an arrow from a bow and, momentarily forgetting caution, ran over to the bank and looked down on the startled faces of Clare and Michael.

'It's the stag!' he exclaimed. 'It's the white stag! It's there! On the floor! It seems to be sleeping! Or drugged! There's no one there. Come and see!'

He sped off again, with Clare and Michael running at his heels.

They crowded into the bothy and looked down at the stag. Gavin felt a deep sense of pity for it, such a splendid beast dumped on the floor of a hut and covered with a dirty tarpaulin. It should be on the hills, wild and free. His anger against the men grew.

Clare knelt down and examined it closely. 'I think it is drugged,' she said. She and Michael then examined it minutely. 'Look!' said Michael. 'There's a bullet wound in its shoulder. It's not bleeding but that would slow it up. I expect they then got close enough to hit it with a dart which drugged it and then gave it another dose once they had got it down.'

Gavin looked at the long gash in the stag's shoulder and he muttered: 'We've got to do something.'

Clare and Michael nodded in agreement.

'It will take some time for Mot to get down and get help,' she said. 'And even longer for Uncle Fergus to get back round here by the track from the Strathyre road. It's quite a way.'

'I wonder if we could hide it?' said Michael. 'It's very heavy, I know, but we could perhaps tug it somewhere?'

'It would be difficult', said Clare. 'It would be very heavy, but it might be done if it was only over a short distance.'

'But they'd catch us if it was only a short distance,' said Gavin.

They thought hard.

'It's still the best chance,' said Clare. 'We'd have a job not leaving tracks, though. But you never know. We might find a sheltered hollow near the bothy and could hide it there. But we'd need to stay with it. We couldn't have hooded crows coming down and pecking its eyes out when it was asleep.'

Gavin agreed. He shivered at the thought of hooded crows, the grey-backed scavenger birds of the Highlands, always ready to swoop on some helpless or ill animal.

'There's a lot of junk behind this partition, Clare,' he said. 'We might find something we could drag it on, old tarpaulins or something of that kind or old rope.'

'That's a good idea,' said Michael. 'But here's a lucky break. This tarpaulin they've used as a cover has holes in the corners with rings: that means we can put a rope through these and tug quite hard without the tarpaulin ripping or tearing.'

They discussed possible plans for a moment or two and then Clare said: 'I'll go and take a look around. We should really keep an eye on the track. When I come back you take a turn at being the sentry, Gavin.'

She went out of the front door and sat down behind a little knoll, keeping out of sight but still able to see the track through the heather stretching away across the moorland.

'I wonder why they didn't lock the door and hide the key,' said Gavin to Michael. 'Yes, that puzzled me, too,' he said. 'They've probably found out that no one uses this place now and they would be safe for a day or two. The door was always locked in the past just to keep the sheep out and to stop them from making a mess inside, but the key was always hidden above the door. I expect whoever was last out forgot to put it back.'

Then his tone changed.

'Or maybe they intended to be quickly back and didn't take the trouble to hang it up.'

He and Gavin looked apprehensively at one another. At that moment Clare came in. 'All clear,' she said. 'You take a turn, Gavin, while I have a chat to Michael about what we might do.'

Gavin clambered up beside the knoll and looked across the winding track, old and rutted, and partly covered in rushes and with odd stones sticking up here and there. An ordinary car couldn't get up that, he knew.

Then his eyes caught a movement high up in the sky and he saw a bird, a tiny speck, very high up in the blue sky, slowly circling, higher than he had ever seen any other bird. He put his binoculars on to it.

He could see large wings, splayed-out wing-tips and he felt by its size it was a golden eagle. Despite all their worries, he felt a sense of gratitude at being in such a place and seeing such a sight.

He was so absorbed that he took his eyes off the track for several minutes and he was just about to call to the bothy for the others to come out and see the eagle when something suddenly glittered brightly down the track.

Round the corner came a group of men, walking briskly towards him. Frantically, he focused his binoculars on them, the eagle temporarily forgotten. He could see they looked very much like the poachers. It certainly wasn't Uncle Fergus. Then he was sure it was them.

He dropped down from the knoll and ran to the bothy.

'They're back!' he called frantically. Clare and Michael looked at him with alarmed faces.

'They're walking here. But they'll be here in a few minutes.'

It was Clare who saved the situation.

'Quick!' she said. 'Behind the partition! We'll hide and they may not see us.'

Gavin and Michael darted behind the old wooden partition and crouched behind an old table and large pieces of wood until they were completely out of sight.

'Hope they don't have a dog with them,' whispered Michael. 'It would sniff us out in seconds.'

'No, I didn't see one,' said Gavin. He peered out. Clare was crouching down with an old piece of newspaper rubbing at bits of the floor.

'What are you doing, Clare?' he said urgently. 'They'll be here in a second. Quick, get in here!'

'All right, I'm on my way,' said Clare. 'I'm just rubbing out our tracks. This place is so dusty they'll realise someone has been here.'

She ducked in behind another pile of wood and they sat silently, with bated breath, listening intently for the sound of voices and steps approaching the door.

Gavin stiffened and could not stop giving a quick look round the partition when the sound of voices did come. The dust that Clare had wiped with the paper had settled again and he took comfort in the fact that no one could see any traces of any other person coming in.

The door lock rattled and the voices sounded angry.

'I thought I told you to lock this door,' said one voice.

'I did lock it, Buck,' replied another. 'I'll swear I did.'

'Well, it's not locked now,' said the man called Buck.

'And I asked you to put the key above the door.'

'I know, Buck,' said the other. 'But it was in the door when we arrived and we wanted to leave the place looking exactly as we found it in case anyone got suspicious.

'There's nothing in these old huts anyway. They only lock the door to keep the sheep out.'

The children crouched still as mice as the men, four in all, crowded inside the room, but Gavin thought there was still one outside.

'Well, no one's here,' said the man called Buck. 'The place is still thick with dust. Now let's get to work! And no mistakes mind! I'm fed up with having to come back here.

'You should have done your job properly and given that stag another injection when we were here. That was the whole idea, to have it sound asleep here while we got a better vehicle. I've got enough to think about trying to get us out of here when our transport has broken down without you muddling things up any further by forgetting to give that deer its injection.

'It's no good telling me when we are miles from the bothy and on our way out of here that you weren't sure whether it needed another dose.' His voice rose in anger 'You should have made sure! What a carry-on, a broken-down vehicle and a so-called animal expert who can't remember how many doses are needed and when they were given!'

One of the other men said: 'I thought it had been given another injection, Buck, otherwise it would have been done at the time.'

'Don't give me that!' said Buck. 'You were brought along to see to all that. You're supposed to know about these things, and you're getting paid for it.'

'I thought we were taking the stag with us,' the man said. 'How was I to know the vehicle would break down? It's at least five miles since we left the vehicle. I thought the stag was sufficiently drugged or I'd have brought more stuff with me.'

Buck cut in angrily, 'Don't tell me what I've to do! I give the orders. We took a risk driving here in the first place but it was a fluke we found the stag and we had to hide it in a hurry. This bothy was very handy. And you know yourself we couldn't drag it far. We were very fortunate no one saw us.

'If it wasn't that the cash for this job was so high I'd never take these risks.'

'All right, all right!' said the man.

'And another thing,' said Buck. 'We took a risk driving here in daylight and we'll be taking a risk coming back and I don't want any more errors. Bring another dose with you.

'We know this bothy is never used, but vehicles on this track in daylight would attract comment. If anyone asks us we were simply hillwalkers out for a stroll. The vehicle is well tucked out of sight down the track.

'Now get on with it. We'll get another vehicle and come back.'

There was silence for a few moments other than the men moving around beside the stag. Some dust eddied upwards when the tarpaulin was moved and one of them sneezed.

'This place is filthy.' said Buck. 'Are you finished yet, Peter?'

'Just about,' said the man called Peter, who had been kneeling beside the stag with a small bottle, a cloth and a syringe in his hand. 'It seems to be all right. That wound has cleared up. I've put some ointment on it. We don't want it infected. I don't want to overdo the knock-out dose, but it should be out for a bit more yet.'

'Okay,' said Buck. 'But no more slips! Now let's get back down the glen looking as if we are enjoying our walk.'

'What's the plan, Buck?' said another voice.

'All right,' said Buck. 'It's quite straightforward. We walk back down the glen, looking very innocent, and get out of here on to the road as quickly as possible.

'If we are stopped when we are in the other vehicle later on we pretend we are tourists who accidentally turned up a hill track thinking it was for public use. Some of them do that anyway.

'If we are stopped on the track now, we are hillwalkers out for a stroll. Leave the talking to me.'

The men grunted agreement.

Then Buck went on. 'Three of us will come back here later with a horsebox. That won't attract comment on the road. It will have fake number plates and dim lights.

'You, John, and Bill, will wait on the main road with another vehicle in case we need a back-up or run into trouble.

'Once we get the stag on to the main road we head for our employer's house. After that he takes over. He will fly the stag out to France and from there to North America, either Canada or the States.'

'When do we get paid?' said a voice.

'When the stag is safely delivered to our man,' said Buck. 'But we are all on expenses as well, so there will be a good pay-out at the end of this.

'Now, cover that stag up again, but leave its head clear.'

The children could hear the men's feet clumping around the stone floor of the bothy, and then Buck said, 'Right, let's go. And lock the door this time!'

'Sure thing, Buck,' came the reply.

The footsteps went outside and the door closed with a little click.

The key turned in the lock and there was a rattle as it was removed on the other side.

Then came a rustling sound as Buck put the key out of sight on a ledge above the door, and the children jumped when he gave the door a rattle.

'That's it!' he said. 'I've put the key where we can easily get it later, just above the door.

'Let's go.'

The Clan sat very still for several minutes until the footsteps and voices receded, the only sound being the steady breathing of the stag on the floor.

'Clare!' whispered Gavin in alarm. 'We're locked in.'

Locked In

'We've got to get out of here,' said Clare.

She rattled the door handle and peered at the lock. 'It's no good trying to force the door,' she said. 'It's far too strong.'

'The window!' said Gavin. 'Try the window.'

They crowded over to that wall and looked up at the tiny window high on one wall and set deeply into the stones.

Michael dragged a box from the back of the bothy, sending up clouds of dust as he did so, and clambered up.

He called down. 'We could break the glass but it wouldn't be any good. The panes are tiny and there's a very strong cross-piece set right across. I don't think we could knock it out with anything. It's very strong and the glass panes are so small we couldn't get through there even if we did break it.'

He paused for breath and then went on: 'They made these windows small on purpose so that storms wouldn't break the panes, or birds or any unwanted people get in on the few occasions the place would be locked.'

He clambered down, breathing heavily.

'Right,' said Clare. 'Spread out everyone. Look for big boxes and so on and we'll see if we can get through the roof. There's no way out through the floor, that's for sure. It's all stone.'

Gavin and Michael dragged more boxes and an old table from behind the back partition, taking as much care as they could not to disturb the stag or cause it harm by sending up clouds of dust. Gradually, they built a rickety tower of junk, the old table with a series of boxes heaped on it, and Gavin volunteered to climb up as he was, in Mot's absence, the lightest.

Michael steadied the boxes as Gavin clambered as high as he could. The pile of junk teetered alarmingly. If he stretched out, Gavin could just touch the roof, dirty and grimy with age. In a few seconds he knew it was hopeless.

He called down. 'It's all boarded up and there are no gaps or cracks. It seems strong. I can't see any of the slates we could see from the outside.'

'You'd better come down,' said Clare. 'It was a good try, Gavin, but any minute that pile will fall and you with it.'

'Yes, this bothy is in good condition,' said Michael. 'It's dry other than a patch near the door, and there would be damp if there were any big gaps in the door or roof.'

He and Gavin slowly dismantled their tower of junk and put it back exactly as they found it and did their best to waft some dust over it again, using an old newspaper.

'A Council of War!' said Clare. 'Gather round! We need ideas.'

They sat down on the floor and looked at one another. Gavin kept glancing at the stag, so peaceful and magnificent, and yet a prisoner, and he was determined it should go free, too.

'It's a pity they didn't leave the key in the door,' said Michael. 'We could have poked it out and perhaps hooked it back under the door with a piece of wire or something.'

Gavin thought hard for a few seconds.

'Wait a minute!' he said. 'I've got an idea! If they put the key above the door we might be able to dislodge it by vibration and drag it in. We could use a sheet of newspaper. Come on, let's have a look.'

They hurried over to the door and examined it closely.

There was a very small space beneath the door, perhaps just large enough to take a key, but it would be a chancy business.

'Great idea, Gavin,' said Clare. 'Get some sheets of newspaper.'

The boys raked around until they found some papers, yellow with age and grimy with dust.

Clare spread out the sheets and slid a couple under the door and pushed them through until there were only tiny pieces on their side.

She lay down and tried to look through the crack, but in vain. She got up with one side of her face all dust and said: 'Can't see a thing! We'll just have to hope it's all right.

'What do you suggest, Gavin? It's your idea.'

Gavin pondered for a second.

'I think we all want to bash against the door with our shoulders and try and dislodge the key from up above. But if we do it too hard it could fall off and perhaps bounce clear of the newspaper. Let's try a couple of shoves until we are clear how much force is needed.'

'Agreed,' said Clare.

They stood close to the door and Clare said: 'Now when I say "bump", all bump against the door together. Now! Bump!'

They all thudded against the door with their shoulders. The door hardly stirred.

'Clare, I think we should bash the sides of the door as well,' said Gavin. 'If the key is above the door we will need to get the vibration going up the sides of the supports, so to speak, rather than the door itself.'

'Quite right,' said Clare. 'I was only testing! Gavin, you take that support, Michael, you take the other. I'll take the door itself. When I say "bash!", crash into it with your shoulders. And hard! Now . . . Bash!'

Three shoulders thudded with all their might into the door and its supports and it quivered and shook.

'Good!' said Clare. 'That seemed just right. Now, once more. Bash!'

They thudded it again.

The door again shook and creaked and there was a muffled 'clink' from outside.

'We've done it!' said Gavin. 'We've dislodged it!'

They carefully drew in the sheets of newspapers until they heard the key make a little noise as it came up against the door.

'Careful now,' said Clare. 'The only decent gap is in the middle of the door. Work it along.'

They carefully tugged and worked at the newspapers until the key seemed to be just opposite the crack at the bottom of the door.

Then, with bated breath, Clare carefully drew the sheets through and, suddenly, there was the key lying on their side of the door.

The Clan leaped to their feet and cheered, capering and dancing around and clapping one another on the back.

'Creag an Sgairbh!' said Clare, holding the key aloft in triumph.

'Creag an Sgairbh!' they chorused back.

They unlocked the door and gleefully trotted out into the open air.

'Whew! What a fright that was,' said Clare. 'Good thinking, Gavin.'

'Yes, great idea,' added Michael.

Gavin glowed with pleasure.

'Och, it was nothing,' he said. 'We all did it.'

'But what do we do now? These men will be back here soon. We can't be sure Uncle Fergus will be here before that,' said Michael.

'We've got to save the stag,' replied Gavin firmly.

Clare looked at the two taut faces and said. 'Yes, we must. We've got no choice. We've got to try and hide it. And I've got a plan of how to do it.

'It'll be hard going. It's likely Uncle Fergus will be here soon but we don't know that for certain.

'The men could come back. They almost bungled things once and they could change their minds again.'

'That's true, Clare,' said Michael. 'But it's a very heavy stag. I don't think we could carry or tug it far. But I agree we've got to try.'

'But what about tracks?' said Gavin. 'We'll leave marks! It's so heavy! They'll see where we have dragged it and simply follow that up and find us.'

Clare nodded. 'Yes, I've thought of that. We've got to decoy them away to give us a chance. After all, we need time. If we can hold them up or delay them then

Uncle Fergus will soon be here.'

'And there's another thing,' chimed in Gavin. 'They had to come back and give the stag another injection. They may have made another mistake there as well. It could wake up before that and then get in a panic when it realises it's in a hut and perhaps it might crash around and hurt itself.'

'It might wake up when they've got it and try and run away and they might even shoot it then.'

Clare called them to order: 'Quiet, you two! Everything you say is correct but I've been thinking hard and here's my plan.

'Let me finish and then tell me what you think of it.'

Gavin and Michael fell silent and looked at her with expectant faces.

Clare went on. 'We'll put the stag on that old tarpaulin, tie pieces of rope to the rings and try and fold it over the stag, like a kind of bed, which we can tug along the ground. There's a couple of old blankets down the back there in the bothy and we can use them for padding. We've got to be sure we don't hurt it when we move it, and we've got to be very careful that we don't harm its eyes. And we've got to be sure it can breathe properly.'

Gavin and Michael nodded agreement and Gavin again felt his anger mount at the thought of the magnificent stag, now so helpless.

'Go on, Clare,' he said.

Clare continued. 'We'll tug it over the moor until we find a decent hollow and then we'll hide it with heather. I'll stay with it, but under cover until help arrives.'

Gavin and Michael began to protest that they should stay as they felt Clare was being placed in danger.

'No, I'll stay!' said Clare. 'I'm the chief and in emergencies I give the orders. It's nice of you two to be concerned but you've got a dangerous task as well. We'll tug the stag across the thickest heather so that it springs back and leaves little or no traces and we'll do our best to wipe out any tracks we might leave. But we'll need to be quick with this as we haven't too much time.'

'Too right!' said Michael. 'But what do you want us to do?'

'I want you and Gavin to make a decoy,' said Clare. 'Get a couple of old logs, or the old table, or something heavy, wrap it in another tarpaulin and tug it out of the bothy door, leaving as many marks as possible. Then tug your load to the side of the track and leave marks showing where you have taken to the moor. But make that the opposite side of the track from me! You've got to ensure they follow you. You've *got* to gain time so that Mot can get Uncle Fergus here. If they catch up on you, you can drop the lot and run, but in different directions. Work your way back here to me. But lose them! They won't expect that and we should stick together as a group wherever possible.

'Well, what do you think of that?'

'Fine!' said Gavin. Trust the resourceful Clare to sort it all out, he thought.

'Yes, good one, Clare,' said Michael.

'All right,' said Clare. 'To work! We'll tackle the stag first.'

They headed back into the bothy and sent up clouds of dust as they raked around and found two old tarpaulins, old rope, and the old blanket.

They spread them on the floor and with much tugging and heaving managed to get the tarpaulins and blankets under the stag until they had made a kind of cradle.

'More blankets,' said Clare, surveying their handiwork. They packed these around the stag until only its legs were sticking out and its head was clear, but with plenty of tarpaulin and a blanket pad underneath.

They stopped for breath, panting hard.

'Will we ever manage to move it, Clare?' said Gavin. 'It's very heavy.'

'I know,' said Clare. 'But it will be easier once we get it to slide. Now, let's pick a route.'

They explored the ground around the bothy and Michael pointed out some firm turf at one side and a smooth slanting stone slab which led up to the heather.

They agreed that was the best route. Gavin clambered up and rolled around on the heather and was relieved to find it long and springy.

'Some heather is burned to keep it short,' said Clare. 'It helps the young grouse, but this lot hasn't been touched for years. That'll be a help!'

Gavin walked across the moor until he came to a little hollow with a tiny rowan tree growing at one edge. The bottom was firm and dry and he thought it would be ideal.

'How about this, Clare?' he called.

Clare and Michael hurried over and inspected it.

'Just right,' said Clare. 'You could walk past this and never see it.'

Then the long haul began. Gavin never forgot it. The stag seemed beyond their strength.

They had got it out of the hut all right, but were panting and soaked in perspiration before they had even achieved that.

Gavin and Michael tugged at the ropes like horses in a harness and Clare pushed at the back and called to them to stop if the stag seemed to be in danger of getting hurt. But bit by bit, tugging and sliding, they worked it round the side of the hut until they reached the firm turf and the slab.

Gavin later thought it was like one of these films where the Egyptian slaves are tugging huge blocks of stone up the pyramids. He and Michael steadily pulled the heavy bundle upwards, with Clare pushing from below. It wasn't a long haul, only a few feet and the angle was a gentle and easy one, but the weight of the stag was almost beyond them.

Clare called: 'Heave! Heave!' and they tugged and pushed and gained a few more inches.

More heaves and more stops until the stag cleared the top of the stone and was on to the heather.

Clare, Michael and Gavin collapsed, lungs panting, arms sore, heads reeling and they lay there for several minutes until the blood stopped pounding in their ears and they felt less dizzy.

Fortunately, their task now became more easy. There was a slight tilt to the ground which was in their favour and the heather seemed to 'lean' their way, but it still seemed ages before they reached the hollow and slid the stag into it.

Clare examined it closely.

'It seems to be all right,' she said. 'It's breathing steadily. Perhaps that stuff they gave it wasn't as strong as they thought or they gave it the wrong dose because it seemed to give a couple of kicks when we were tugging it. But it seems sound asleep now.'

Gavin and Michael bent anxiously over the stag, its

silver-grey body now partly shrouded in the deep heather. Its sides rose and fell steadily.

'It's all right,' said Michael. 'Let's get busy.'

He and Gavin began to tug out heather by the roots. Sometimes Gavin slashed at tougher roots with his knife but it was better to tug and pull as that left fewer marks.

Soon they had a great pile. Clare urged them to spread out and they were careful not to take heather from only one corner.

Clare decided to leave the stag on the tarpaulin as it helped hide its whiteness, but loosened it so the beast could breathe freely. She left one corner free so she could sit on it and not catch damp from the ground.

'Now we need a decent cover,' she said.

'I'll make myself comfortable and you have to lace me in so that the surface of the moor looks natural.'

Gavin and Michael began to place the heather as a kind of roof over the stag and Clare.

'Wait a minute,' she said, fumbling in her rucksack. She produced a little tube. 'Anti-midge cream!' she said with a grin. 'They'll be murder later on.'

She dabbed her face, neck, hands and wrists, took an old green hat from out of a side pocket, pulled that well down on her head, and sat down beside the stag and made herself comfortable against the side of the hollow.

'Your face is a bit pale, Clare' said Gavin.

'Good man, Gav,' she said, and smeared some peat-moss over her face.

'Now off you go, you two, and get busy with the decoy. I'll be all right. Check the heather going back and make sure we haven't left any tracks.'

The boys laid in some more heather, trying to make it as natural as possible and Clare helped thread it upright.

In a few minutes she and the stag were well hidden.

Gavin walked past a few paces away to try it out and called: 'It's working, Clare. No one would see you unless they stumbled over you.'

'Thanks!' said Clare. 'Now get on with phase two of the plan. I'll be all right. I'll doze. Rather nice really, sitting back here in comfort. If you do have to come back, remember to give the curlew call.'

'Goodbye,' said the boys together, and hurried back across the moor, occasionally kicking or tugging at bits of heather to put them upright again.

But it looked all right and only a very expert eye would know that a heavy object had been slid across the ground.

Once back at the bothy, Gavin and Michael got busy again. They tugged out the old table, put it in a tarpaulin, added a heavy log which had been used as a kind of seat, wrapped it all in the tarpaulin and tugged it out of the door.

'Here's a good bit,' said Gavin, pointing to a marshy piece of ground to the side of the bothy.

'Yes, that'll do,' said Michael, and they wearily tugged their load through the water and rushes leaving a wide and satisfactory trail.

'Here's a lucky break,' said Gavin pointing to a little burn on the opposite side of the track from the side where Clare was hidden and which ran across part of the moor, fringed on each side by peat hags and heather.

Its sides were also marshy, and they happily tugged

their bundle along it and found that, unlike the heavy stag on the heather, the wet ground made the table and log slide along more easily.

'Whew!' said Gavin, sitting down and mopping his brow. 'This is hard going! But we're managing.'

'Yes, we are,' replied Michael. 'We'll tug it further away still, though. Let's get back to the bothy and tidy up the pile behind the partition. We don't want them to spot we've taken items.'

'I don't suppose they checked it too carefully,' said Gavin. 'The dust was pretty thick. But we can spread it around again.'

They re-arranged the pile of junk behind the partition and then used an old broom and newspapers to send clouds of dust swirling around the bothy until it settled satisfactorily over all the rubbish and over themselves.

'Here's a find!' said Gavin, holding up an old pair of boots with nailed soles. 'Let's baffle them by leaving lots of prints!'

So he and Michael took it in turn to put on the large boots and stamp around on the mucky bits of ground until they left prints all over the place.

'Come on,' said Michael. 'Let's do some more tugging.'

'Good idea!' laughed Gavin.

They tugged and hauled for about an hour until they had made an unmistakable swathe through the rushes and tall grasses and then went back and stamped on every bit of muddy ground they could find. By this time the bothy was out of sight over the rises in the moorland.

Finally, they came to a halt and collapsed beside a

little heather-covered mound.

'Michael!' said Gavin. 'I'm whacked. I can't do any more.'

'I know,' said Michael. 'So am I, but we've done all we can. It will delay them a little, give Clare a chance and gain some time for Uncle Fergus to get here.

'We've done all we can. So let them come!'

*　　*　　*　　*

And they did come. It was Clare who later filled in the details because she could just see the bothy by carefully lifting her head and she could also see the track. A vehicle had bumped up it. The men jumped out at the bothy and went inside.

'They came running out again,' she told Gavin, Michael and Mot later, 'like wasps out of a nest after it has been rattled with a stick. I kept very still and they seemed to be in a panic.

'They stood up on high bits and looked around and I thought I was done for. Then one of them saw your tracks and they started to run after you. But one of them called the others back and they began arguing.

'Then they began to search around properly and they again set off after you. Just at that point a police Land Rover and another car came up the glen and they all scattered, leaving their vehicle.

'The police chased them and some of them were caught. But three got away, including their leader. Uncle Fergus says the police will get them, though, as there are road blocks now on every road.

'They can't get far. The police have both their

vehicles, including one which had broken down.'

She paused for breath. They were all gathered by the shore of the lochan and were about to spend the day on the island, Uncle Fergus and Aunt Elspeth having forbidden all wandering until the rest of the men were caught.

'And the stag?' said Gavin urgently. 'What about the stag? Did it get away?'

Clare said quietly, 'I didn't tell you before this because I'm worried about it. It may still be in danger. I was just about to get to my feet and shout to Uncle Fergus when the stag got up. It had been moving a bit before then and that had me really worried because I thought it might give our hiding place away or it might try and run away just at the time when the men were here.

'But it eventually got to its feet and clambered out of the hollow. It lurched around a bit and then it set off across the moor.'

'Where?' asked Michael. 'Where did it go? In which direction?'

'I don't know for sure,' said Clare. 'There was so much happening. One minute I was trying to see it didn't hurt itself or me and the next I was trying to see what the men were doing and trying to stay hidden at the same time. And then Uncle Fergus and the police arrived.

'When I next looked round it was trying to gallop across the moor. I think it was still partly doped. It was swaying and sometimes it fell down. I tried to follow its tracks but the heather is very thick.'

She paused again, clearly upset.

'Never mind, Clare,' said Gavin gently. 'You did

everything you could. It was your plan that saved it and gave us time to get help here. It will be all right. These men obviously made mistakes with the amount of drug they should have given it.'

Mot and Michael nodded agreement.

'We can get on with the hut today,' said Mot. 'It's time we did that anyway.

'We can't do anything more about the stag except keep our eyes open and hope it will be all right.'

'Yes, that's right,' said Gavin. 'Come on, Clare, no moping.'

'We're all a bit tired,' added Michael. 'A nice restful day is what I need.'

So they got the birlinn and galley out and paddled over to the island and spent the day finishing off their den in the ruins until it was firm and snug and would keep the rain out and yet was well hidden from prying eyes.

They went home early, eager for sleep.

No sooner had the sound of their paddles in the water receded than on the hillside above the loch, a white, swaying figure slowly descended the steep heather, grass and rocks, sometimes lying down for many minutes, twice falling and rolling downhill in a great clatter of stones, then clumsily lurching to its feet and continuing on until it reached the shore of the lochan and collapsed.

Its great antlers tilted wearily forward, its hooves lay in the shallows and its eyes were heavy with exhaustion.

It lay there for many minutes before slowly getting to its feet and wading deep into the lochan.

It stood there, swaying slightly, but the cool water was reviving it and after a pause it began to swim steadily for the island.

CHAPTER 11

The White Stag Returns

'Yippee!' yelled Clare the next day, momentarily forgetting their rule about quiet, as the galley forged out once more for the island.

The sun still shone, the sky was blue, the hillsides green and it was clearly going to be another of these days which can be all too rare in Scotland, but when they come they are like jewels.

They felt the heat of the sun on their shirts as the water broke beneath their paddles and the island neared. They pulled into the little inlet and hauled the birlinn and galley ashore.

Clare was the first into the courtyard and the first back out again.

Her voice broke with excitement as she held up her hand for the boys to halt. 'Stop!' she said dramatically and they knew by her tone she had momentous news.

'What is it, Clare?' said Gavin. 'What on earth is the matter?'

'Yes, come on, Clare,' said Michael. 'Out of the way! What have you found in there, a dead body?'

'No, a live one,' gasped Clare. 'It's the stag!'

'The stag? Rubbish!' said Mot. 'You're having us on.'

'Come and look,' said Clare and led the way into their den. There, lying quietly inside, was the stag.

Its sides rose and fell as it steadily breathed, its eyes looked large and dark and somehow appealing. 'It was as if it was trying to tell us it needed help,' Gavin said afterwards.

But it still looked dozy and sleepy.

'I expect the drug is still having an effect,' said Clare. 'It must have been looking for a refuge and swam over to the island and then crawled in here because it looked dark and safe.'

The Clan stood looking at it in silence for some moments and the stag's eyes closed again.

'Come on,' whispered Clare and they tip-toed out into the sunny court-yard again.

'What are we to do?' said Gavin.

'The men might come and find it. After all, they came and looked at the island for a long time and they might have been thinking of it as a hiding place like the bothy.'

'True,' said Mot. 'One of us had better get back and tell Uncle Fergus and then we can get a guard mounted until the drug wears off.'

'It might get in a panic if it wakes up properly,' said Clare. 'We should make it some bedding first. But be careful, if it starts to thrash around we could be in real danger. It'll only take a minute.'

So they broke their rule about not disturbing the island's undergrowth too much and got huge bunches of ferns and packed them round the stag, making it a kind of bed.

'One more thing,' said Clare. 'If it didn't leave any tracks in here then there is no way of the men knowing it's here. So we should be safe until Uncle Fergus gets here.'

'Will I go over and have a look?' said Mot.

'All right,' said Clare. 'But be quick. We don't want to waste too much time.'

They sat down in the courtyard while Mot got the birlinn out and paddled over to the far shore.

'Don't show yourselves unnecessarily,' said Clare. 'It's better to be on the safe side.'

So they watched through the chinks in the stone work as Mot reached the far shore and pulled the birlinn up among some rocks.

Mot bent down and carefully examined the shore-line, moving along until he suddenly stopped at some clear prints in a little patch of sand. They were clearly deer prints.

He followed them along a little as they fringed the shore and stopped beside a large boulder to examine some which looked slightly blurred.

At that moment a man's hand descended on his shoulder.

'Got you, you little swine!', said a rough voice.

Mot acted instantly. Just as the hand grabbed him and the man leaned forward over him he twisted and bent his body.

The force of the man's body took him over Mot's bent back and as Mot wriggled free the man landed with a thud, partly on the shore and partly in the water, causing a crashing splash that Gavin and the others heard on the island.

Mot was clever. Instead of running along the shore

where another man waited to block his passage, he immediately turned up hill, frantically and nimbly scrambling through the ferns and over boulders, higher and higher until he had left the men and their shouts behind.

He halted, panting, and looked across to the island where Clare and the others, concealment forgotten, stared anxiously at him.

He lifted his hand in salute to show he was all right and then held out his left arm stiffly to let them know he was going for help and the direction he would take.

Gavin, Clare and Michael all waved back, and he set off at a fast run, the product of many hours on the hill where he could trot quite fast while at the same time looking out for awkward bits without slowing his pace.

Meanwhile, Clare, Gavin and Michael conferred anxiously.

'It'll take him some time to get round,' said Clare, tautly. 'It's a long way, right round the head of the loch. One of us should go over to the other bank, the way we always come. That's the quickest!'

'But they could come here!' said Gavin. 'Two of us couldn't do much, but three of us might do something.'

'What can we do?' said Michael. 'There's three of them, don't forget. That's what Uncle Fergus said — three got away at the bothy! And for all we know there may be more of them. They've had time to get more men!'

Clare thought for a moment: 'You're right,' she said. 'We've no time. One of us must get help. Michael, you're the fastest runner. Take the galley and paddle like mad!'

Michael began to protest that he didn't want to leave

them, but Clare cut him short.

'Don't argue!' she said. 'We've no time. Speed is the thing. Off you go!'

'Yes, go!' said Gavin. 'We'll be all right.' (He didn't really think so, but he put a good face on it.)

'Shouldn't we all go?' said Michael. 'It would mean leaving the stag but it's sound asleep again and they won't harm it. I don't like leaving you here.'

'No!' said Clare. 'They're not sure who is here, but they could have seen the stag going over. They may even have come over and seen it and then removed themselves when they realised we were coming.

'So long as we are here and make a noise it might slow them up and worry them.'

'Yes, that's a good point,' said Gavin hurriedly. 'Every minute gained helps us and hinders them. You'd better go, Michael.'

'Yes, no more talking,' said Clare.

'All right, Clare,' said Michael, mind made up. 'If that's the way you want it.'

'Yes, it is,' said Clare, heart pounding. 'You're the fastest.'

Michael said nothing more except to add, 'Look after her, Gavin,' at which Clare snorted. He hurried through the trees to the galley and soon sent it speeding across the loch for the far shore.

Clare and Gavin could see the two men standing on stones gazing at the island, and then one of them went up the hillside a little way.

'He'll soon see Michael's wake,' said Gavin.

'Yes,' said Clare. 'But he'll be well across the loch by that time and they can't stop him now.'

It was then Gavin had a series of brainwaves.

'Let's make it look as if lots of people are here,' he said. 'We could light a large fire with lots of smoke!'

'Great idea!' said Clare. 'Other people might see it and come to see what's on fire. I'll get it going! You get wood, Gavin!'

Gavin frantically raked around in their store and took a few seconds to look at the stag. Its eyes were open again, but looked sleepy and weary, he thought, and it lay quite still.

He returned to the courtyard where Clare had her kindling already alight and she added some more wood.

He noticed she had not lit the fire in the old fireplace but in the middle of a cleared space in the courtyard.

'We've got to get this seen,' she said.

By now the wood was crackling merrily and she added some larger branches from their store, now quite dried out, and the flames soon roared up.

'That ought to do it,' she said. 'Quick, Gavin, get me lots of green ferns and stuff like that.'

Again Gavin went foraging and returned with armfuls of ferns. Clare put a bundle of these on the fire and the flames died for a minute and then a thick pillar of grey, choking smoke rose straight up and stood out clearly in the still air.

'Yippee!' said Gavin, piling on more.

'Steady on!' said Clare. 'We don't want to choke it.'

She poked around underneath with a stick, raising the pile of ferns until the flames had a chance to roar up again and then re-stacked the fire.

The smoke billowed up in the most satisfactory way, reaching higher and higher.

'Gosh!' said Gavin. 'You could see that from the road.'

He paused, then said: 'Now, let's put our balmorals on sticks and show them over the walls so they'll think there are more of us. We could dart around, keeping low and then showing ourselves, and try and puzzle them. That might help.'

'Yes, it would!' said Clare. 'Come on!'

She piled some more wood and ferns on the fire and the column of smoke billowed up once more.

They went to the walls and stood obviously in view of the men on the far shore and then ducked down.

They crawled along out of sight, put their balmorals on sticks and raised them to the head of the wall and then gradually lowered them again. They did this from several points and then halted for breath.

Then Gavin remembered an old story of a great warrior of the Clan Donald, Somerled, the Lord of the Isles, who deceived his enemies into thinking he had three armies whereas he only had one, by getting them to march round the side of a hill wearing different clothes in turn.

'Let's put on our cagoules or jerseys and show ourselves again,' said Gavin. 'That might baffle them further.'

So they did that, too, changing garments and darting past open sections in the wall, sometimes breaking off to build up the fire, trying to give the impression of several people being on the island.

They banged their dixies and tins and shouted *'Creag an Sgairbh!'* together and then singly at different parts of the castle, only stopping when the stag raised its head and looked at them with eyes which now showed a new brightness.

They waved the top of their stakes over the walls,

singly and then in pairs, and at different points and they added more wood and ferns to the fire and when they could do no more they flopped in the courtyard, exhausted and panting.

'I think that's halted them for a bit,' whispered Gavin.

He and Clare could just see the far shore through cracks in the stonework but there was no sign of the men.

'Do you think they've gone?' Clare said.

Then she and Gavin suddenly sat upright.

From the far end of the loch came the sound of a boat engine.

The Siege of the Castle

Gavin leaped to the walls, caution forgotten.

There, coming towards them, was what looked like a large boat with four men inside.

'It's them, Clare!' he said. 'It's the poachers! They'll be here in a few minutes. What'll we do? What *can* we do?'

Clare clambered up beside him and together they saw to their horror a large, inflatable boat which had an outboard engine attached at the rear. It wasn't fast, but it came steadily on, engine throbbing, and it was certainly big enough to take the stag away.

'They must have some kind of vehicle quite close to the loch to get that boat down here,' said Clare, angrily. 'It's probably got a roof rack. Do you think we should go, Gavin. We could try and wade or partly swim across and probably get to the shore just as they were landing on the other side.

'They probably wouldn't bother chasing us. It's the stag they want, not us. Oh, I do wish Uncle Fergus would get here now! We almost had them beaten, and now they're going to get away!'

The boat came closer to the island and Clare and Gavin could see that it was going to pass below the castle walls at a point where the loch was quite deep and where the walls rose almost sheer from the brown water.

'They don't know about the inlet,' said Gavin. 'That's a break! If we have to leave we can push off from there when they get to the other side. We'll get a minute or two because it is quite hard to land on that side as the rocks are steep.'

'We can't hide on the island, it's too small,' whispered Clare, her mind racing over a number of possibilities.

'We could dodge them in the trees but not for long. There's four of them!'

'Perhaps we could try and wreck their boat,' muttered Gavin. 'Pull the plug out or something. We *must* try.'

They gazed in distress and anger as the boat slowed a little to come round the corner of the island.

In a few minutes it would pass beneath them.

'We'd better get into the dungeon tower,' said Clare. 'It's only got one entrance and it is small. They might leave us alone there.'

'Yes,' said Gavin, sadly. 'We can try and whack anyone with our staves who tries to duck underneath. There's a corner we could wedge ourselves in. They'd have a job getting us out of there.'

They looked at one another, almost on the verge of tears. In the courtyard their fire still crackled but the long column of smoke had by now died down.

Of the stag, there was no sign, and they hoped it was still asleep.

Then inspiration struck Gavin. 'Creag an Sgairbh,' he said quietly. 'I've got it! We'll sink them!'

He fumbled in his pocket and pulled out the head of

the old salmon spear that they had found earlier in the castle.

'Michael loaned it to me the other day,' he said. 'I thought I would try and make a shaft for it. Quick, give me your staff, Clare,' he said urgently. 'It's got a narrower point than mine.'

Clare quickly handed it over and Gavin worked the point into the hole at the edge of the spear-head. He worked with desperate speed and slightly nicked one of his fingers because the spear-head was so sharp. 'Ouch,' he said, as he worked on.

He placed the blade in a little crack in the rock so the edges held it tightly and pushed on the staff with all his might until it was firmly lodged in the socket of the spear-head.

'Great!' said Clare. 'What next?'

Gavin's mind worked with lightning speed. 'Clare, get up on that ledge and peer over the battlements. When they are just about to pass that little arrow slit at the bottom of the wall, tell me! I'll stick the spear through and the blade might puncture the side of their boat as they go past.'

'Great!' said Clare for a second time. 'You're a genius!'

She sprang on to a block of stone and clambered on to the wall and peered over. 'Quick, Gavin!' she said. 'They are getting very near.'

Gavin hurried down to the base of the wall and peered through the tiny slit. It was just above water level and he knelt down and held the salmon spear just at the edge. He couldn't see much, just the water and the far-off shore.

'Get ready, Gavin,' hissed Clare. 'Here they come!'

Gavin's heart thudded as he waited, poised. Then Clare called again, 'Get ready . . . NOW!!!'.

Gavin pushed the spear through the slit with all his strength just as the grey bow of the boat passed him.

The spear went right into its side and the momentum of the boat swung him round, but the edges of the slit steadied the shaft and he held on. The blade ran along the length of the boat and there was a ripping, tearing noise as air rushed out. The boat tipped and water began to pour in. Surprised shouts rent the air.

The spear came free, and Gavin, still clutching it, clambered up the wall beside Clare and looked over.

As they watched awestruck, the boat began to sink and the men were soon floundering in the deep water amid oars, boxes and other gear. Cries of alarm and anger ran out.

Gavin and Clare turned to one another in delight and elation.

They literally danced on the parapet.

'Creag an Sgairbh!' they roared in triumph.

No matter what was to happen to them now, the stag was safe from being carried away.

They had won precious time.

But they were not out of danger yet.

The men clambered up the rocks, wet and dripping, and began to scramble and wade along the foot of the castle wall until they could get ashore into the trees.

Gavin and Clare raced into the courtyard, still holding their staves, and climbed down into the ruins of the little dungeon tower.

There they ducked through a very low doorway, which made passage for a grown-up difficult, and crouched behind two large blocks of stone just inside the entrance. They gripped their staves in the semi-darkness and got ready to lash out at anyone trying to come through.

They were shivering with excitement and apprehension, but for a long time they heard nothing. They crouched anxiously, waiting.

The men were soaked and demoralised and were quarrelling over what to do next. Then they began to search the island to see if the children had left a boat anywhere, but Mot had taken the birlinn and Michael had the galley.

They didn't know the lochan well enough to realise that one could wade across it with difficulty, if one knew where the shallow bits were.

They had a cursory look for the children, but the remnants of the fire attracted them and they spent some time trying to get the flames to burn up as they huddled round it, wet clothes steaming. They found the stag but left it alone, although it did cause a babble of talk among them.

Clare and Gavin thought these minutes would never end. They had no idea what was happening. They only knew that the men could not get off the island and that they had to stay free until help arrived.

After a bit, an enraged Buck called his three helpers together and suggested to them that they find the children. They might be able to use the children as hostages, he said, and still get away.

Shivering and shaken they agreed, and began to comb the island. It took them a long while because Buck had no idea how many children there were and, to start with, he thought it was going to be easy.

They beat through grasses and ferns, in the trees and

bushes, among the rocks, and under logs, and then went back to the castle.

'But we've already looked here,' said one of the men. 'Perhaps they had a boat of their own, a canoe, or something like that and have gone.'

'No, they're still here,' said Buck. 'And they're our only chance of getting out of this mess. Check every bit of this ruin. Don't harm them! We want them as a guarantee of safe-conduct out of here.'

They began to systematically check the ruins, even lifting loose stones in case there was an entrance to an underground room.

And eventually they came to the base of the dungeon tower and the little dark doorway and stood gazing at it.

'They're in there,' said Buck. 'I've had enough of this lot. Let's get them out!'

Gavin and Clare shrank back as a man's hand came through the tiny entrance. Then Gavin reacted and smartly whacked it with his stave.

There was a yell and the hand was withdrawn, and angry voices could again be heard outside. Then another man rushed at the tiny entrance and tried to cram himself underneath.

Clare and Gavin, inwardly very frightened, both whacked his hand and shoulders and he withdrew, having partially stuck in the entrance.

'Get Willie!' said a voice. 'He's the smallest. Get him to rush them and the rest of us can grab their poles once he's inside.'

More tension-filled seconds followed and Gavin, pressing back against the wall, suddenly let out a gasp.

'What is it?' said the startled Clare, gripping her stave tightly.

'This stone moved!' said Gavin.

'Look!' He leaned back against a large block at the back of the little alcove and, sure enough, the stone moved.

'It must be on some kind of pivot,' whispered Gavin. 'Look, there's light!'

They could see a tiny glimmer of light at the back.

'Come on, shove!' said Gavin urgently. 'We can get out this way with any luck.'

He and Clare pushed with all their might and the huge block suddenly swung round with a loud grating noise and, with surprised eyes, they found themselves looking out of the back of the castle wall and down at the waters of the lochan.

'Quick, get through,' urged Gavin. He and Clare wriggled through until they were on a little ledge outside the walls, hidden from above by a protruding block of stone.

'It must have been an escape-hole, built long ago,' said Clare. 'They could sneak out, drop down into a boat and be away before anyone noticed.'

'Quick!' said Gavin, his thoughts racing. 'Push the stone back or they'll come through too!'

Frantically, they pushed with all their might and the stone rolled back into place with a loud grating noise. They could hear more angry yells.

'I think Willie got inside only to find us gone,' said Clare, her teeth chattering with cold and excitement.

'They can't touch us here,' said Gavin. 'unless they can move the stone. We'd better sit with our backs against it. The chances are that it is so finely balanced that any pressure the other way will halt it. It must be something like that otherwise it would have stuck permanently over the years.'

They sat anxiously together, backs tightly pressed against the stone, feet braced against a little ledge and staves still tightly grasped. And it was from there, with a great sense of joy, relief and elation, that they saw Uncle Fergus and a group of men arrive at the lochside and wave to them.

They launched boats and Clare and Gavin could see several policemen, and in the middle an excited Mot and Michael who waved their arms. From the top end of the loch came another group of men, forestry workers who had been attracted by the large pillar of smoke.

'Creag an Sgairbh!' Clare and Gavin let rip.

*   *   *   *

Long after, when Gavin was back in London, he occasionally spread out his gear and looked at it, re-living these days. In his room he had his special dirk, his present from his previous holiday and he now added to that his painted stave, a sheep's neck-bone woggle painted black with a little MacRae brooch glued on, and in a little box lined with cotton wool, a long, silver hair from the white stag which he had found in the castle.

He looked out of his window at the night sky, the street lights shining and the lights of traffic glinting and he could just make out some pale stars in the sky.

From the garden and from a park not far away he suddenly caught the scent of wet grass and trees and he was transported back to the island and these eventful days. Willie, Buck and the rest had surrendered without a fight and were taken away. The Ogre had escaped but the police felt he would never risk coming back to Scotland.

When the police took the men on to the boats, the children had raced to the castle only to find the white stag had gone.

Then they heard a loud splashing noise and they saw it swimming steadily across the lochan to the hillside shore. It landed unsteadily, then shook itself and slowly began to climb the steep slopes, gaining energy as it went.

It paused on the top of a knoll and stood there, silver and magnificent, head held high.

The children gasped. 'It's where it should be,' said Gavin, awe-struck.

The white stag looked down at them for a second, then bowed its great head, turned and vanished over the skyline.

They never saw it again.